PUFFIN BOOK

RUSTY RUNS AWAY

Ruskin Bond's first novel, *The Room on the Roof*, written when he was seventeen, received the John Llewellyn Rhys Memorial Prize in 1957. Since then he has written a number of novellas (including *Vagrants in the Valley*, *A Flight of Pigeons* and *Mr Oliver's Diary*), essays, poems and children's books, many of which have been published in Puffin Books. He has also written over 500 short stories and articles that have appeared in magazines and anthologies. He received the Sahitya Akademi Award in 1993, the Padma Shri in 1999 and the Padma Bhushan in 2014.

Ruskin Bond was born in Kasauli, Himachal Pradesh, and grew up in Jamnagar, Dehradun, New Delhi and Simla. As a young man, he spent four years in the Channel Islands and London. He returned to India in 1955. He now lives in Landour, Mussoorie, with his adopted family.

Also in Puffin by Ruskin Bond

RUSKIN BOND

RUSTY

Runs Away

ILLUSTRATIONS BY

ARCHANA SREENIVASAN

PUFFIN BOOKS

An imprint of Penguin Random House

PUFFIN BOOKS

USA | Canada | UK | Ireland | Australia
New Zealand | India | South Africa | China | Singapore

Puffin Books is part of the Penguin Random House group of companies
whose addresses can be found at global.penguinrandomhouse.com

Published by Penguin Random House India Pvt. Ltd
4th Floor, Capital Tower 1, MG Road,
Gurugram 122 002, Haryana, India

First published in Puffin by Penguin Books India 2003
This illustrated edition published 2014

Copyright © Ruskin Bond 2003

ISBN 9780143333395

Typeset in Adobe Garamond Pro by Ram Das Lal, New Delhi

Printed at Manipal Technologies Limited, India

Contents

Contents

Author's Note

HERE WE ARE again, with Rusty and Co.!

My young readers responded kindly to the first 'Rusty' book, and the Puffin editors (good-looking Puffins, all of them) feel sufficiently encouraged to bring out 'Rusty 2'—i.e. *Rusty Runs Away*.

In *Rusty, the Boy from the Hills*, a lot of interesting things happened *around* Rusty. In this volume, exciting things happen *to* him—or rather, he *makes* things happen, first by running away from his school (in the company of the mischievous Daljit), and later by escaping from the strict confines of his guardian's home and finding friendship and adventure with Somi, Ranbir, Kishen and others. And in discovering this new life, the teenaged Rusty also discovers a different kind of India from that in which he grew up.

Once again, I am indebted to Udayan Mitra and Anjana Ramakrishnan for bringing together these episodes from Rusty's life. And to Shubhadarshini Singh for her sensitive adaptation of the stories in her TV serial, *Ek Tha Rusty*.

Landour, Mussoorie   Ruskin Bond
October 2014

The Window

IT WAS SPRING, and I was living with my guardian and his wife at Dehra. Every day, after attending the day-school classes I was free to engage myself in any way I fancied. But I did not have to go out anywhere to occupy myself. I'd simply go upstairs—to my room, it was on the roof—and I'd spend all my free time there.

To be precise, I spent *all* my time at the window. For, from this window I felt as if I owned the world.

But only from the window.

The banyan tree, just opposite, was mine, and its inhabitants my subjects. They were two squirrels, a few mynahs, a crow, and at night, a pair of flying foxes. The squirrels were busy in the afternoons, the birds in the mornings and evenings, the foxes at night. Though I had lots of homework and a lot more to study, I wasn't as busy as the inhabitants of the banyan tree.

1

There was also a mango tree but that came later, in the summer, when I met Koki and the mangoes were ripe.

At first, I was lonely in my room. But then I discovered the power of my window. It looked out on the banyan tree, on the garden, on the broad path that ran beside the building, and out over the roofs of other houses, over roads and fields, as far as the horizon. The path was not a very busy one but it held variety: an *ayah*, with a baby in a pram; the postman, an event in himself; the fruit-seller, the toy-seller, calling their wares in high-pitched familiar cries; the rent-collector; a posse of cyclists; a long chain of schoolgirls; a lame beggar . . . all passed my way, the way of my window . . .

One day, a tonga came rattling and jingling down the path and stopped in front of the house opposite ours. A girl and an elderly lady climbed down, and a servant unloaded their baggage. They went into that house and the tonga moved off, the horse snorting a little.

The next afternoon the girl looked up from her garden and saw me at my window. She had long black hair that fell to her waist, tied with a single red ribbon. Her eyes were black like her hair and just as shiny. She must have been about ten, a year or two younger than me.

3

'Hello,' I said with a friendly smile.

She looked suspiciously at me. 'Who are you?' she asked.

'I'm a ghost.'

She laughed, and her laugh had a gay, mocking quality. 'You look like one!'

I didn't think her remark particularly flattering, but I had asked for it. I stopped smiling anyway.

'What have you got up there?' she asked.

'Magic,' I said.

She laughed again but this time without mockery. 'I don't believe you,' she said.

'Why don't you come up and see for yourself?' My guardian, Mr John Harrison, and his wife were, as usual, at the club. I think they played bridge or something. Anyway, they always returned late if they went out, so there was no fear of being caught at something they didn't approve of—my mixing with Indians.

The girl hesitated a little but came round to the steps of my house and began climbing them, slowly, cautiously. And when she entered my room, she brought a magic of her own.

'Where's your magic?' she asked, looking me in the eye.

'Come here,' I said, and I took her to the window, and showed her the world.

She said nothing but stared out of the window uncomprehendingly at first, and then with increasing interest. And after some time she turned round and smiled at me, and we were friends.

I only knew that her name was Koki, and that she had come with her aunt for the summer months; I didn't ask her anything more about herself, and she didn't ask me any questions either.

Even if she had asked me anything about myself, I'd have nothing interesting to tell her. My name was Rusty, I was of British parentage, and I was twelve years old. I had been born right there—in Dehra—but had no family to speak of. My parents had separated when I was just four, and my mother had remarried. I had spent most of my childhood with my father, and when he travelled because of his job—he worked for a rubber company in Burma—I'd spend my days with my paternal grandparents in their house at Dehra. But my father had passed away suddenly because of malaria and my mother, though she tried to include me in her life again, couldn't really pay much attention to me, as she also had her baby to take care of. I stayed with my grandmother after that but she too passed away all of a sudden. Someone, I think it was one of my aunts, had entrusted me to the care of Mr John Harrison (a cousin of my father) and his wife. They were my guardians now, but I hardly felt the warmth of a family even with them around. That was all I had to say about my life until then. It was hardly worth mentioning.

Koki came up my steps nearly every day, and joined me at the window. There was a lot of excitement to be had in our world, especially when the rains broke.

At the first rumblings, women would rush outside to retrieve the washing on the clothesline and if there was a breeze, to chase a few garments across the compound. When the rain came, it came with a vengeance, making a bog of the garden and a river of the path. A cyclist would come riding furiously down the path, an elderly gentleman would be having difficulty with an umbrella, naked children would be frisking about in the rain. Sometimes Koki would run out on the roof, and shout and dance in the rain. And the rain would come through the open door and window of the room, flooding the floor and making an island of my bed.

But the window was more fun than anything else. It gave us the power of detachment: we were deeply interested in the life around us, but we were not involved in it.

'It is like a cinema,' said Koki. 'The window is the screen, the world is the picture.'

Soon the mangoes were ripe, and Koki was in the

branches of the mango tree as often as she was in my room. From the window I had a good view of the tree, and we spoke to each other from the same height. We ate far too many mangoes, at least five a day.

'Let's make a garden on the roof,' suggested Koki. She was full of ideas like this.

'And how do you propose to do that?' I asked.

'It's easy. We bring up mud and bricks and make the flower beds. Then we plant the seeds. We'll grow all sorts of flowers.'

'The roof will fall in,' I predicted.

But it didn't. We spent two days carrying buckets of mud up the steps to the roof and laying out the flower beds. All this was done in utmost secrecy—when my guardian and his wife were away from home. It was very hard work, but Koki did most of it. When the beds were ready, we had the opening ceremony. Apart from a few small plants collected from the garden below we had only one species of seeds—pumpkin . . . .

We planted the pumpkin seeds in the mud, and felt proud of ourselves.

But it rained heavily that night, and in the morning I discovered that everything—except the bricks—had been washed away.

So we returned to the window.

A mynah had been in a fight—with a crow

perhaps—and the feathers had been knocked off its head. A bougainvillaea that had been climbing the wall had sent a long green shoot in through the window.

Koki said, 'Now we can't shut the window without spoiling the creeper.'

'Then we will never close the window,' I said.

And we let the creeper into the room.

The rains passed, and an autumn wind came whispering through the branches of the banyan tree. There were red leaves on the ground, and the wind picked them up and blew them about, so that they looked like butterflies. I would watch the sun rise in the morning, the sky all red, until its first rays splashed the window-sill and crept up the walls of the room. And in the evening Koki and I watched the sun go down in a sea of fluffy clouds; sometimes the clouds were pink, and sometimes orange; they were always coloured clouds, framed in the window.

'I'm going tomorrow,' said Koki one evening.

I was too surprised to say anything.

'You stay here for ever, don't you?' she said.

I remained silent.

'When I come again next year you will still be here, won't you?'

'I don't know,' I said. I was so used to being uprooted from any place that I called 'home' that I hardly dared to estimate how long I'd be in one place. 'But the window will still be here.'

'Oh, do be here next year,' she said, 'or someone will close the window!'

In the morning the tonga was at the door, and the servant, the aunt and Koki were in it. Koki waved to me at my window. Then the driver flicked the reins, the wheels of the carriage creaked and rattled, the bell jingled. Down the path went the tonga, down the path and through the gate, and all the time Koki waved; and from the gate I must have looked like a ghost, standing alone at the high window, amongst the bougainvillaea.

When the tonga was out of sight I took the sprig of bougainvillaea in my hand and pushed it out of the room. Then I closed the window. It would be opened only when the spring and Koki came again.

The Prospect of Flowers

FERN HILL, THE Oaks, Hunter's Lodge, The Parsonage, The Pines, Dumbarnie, Mackinnon's Hall and Windermere. These are the names of some of the old houses that still stand on the outskirts of Dehra. Most of them have fallen into decay and ruin. They are very old, of course—built over a hundred years ago by Britishers who sought relief from the searing heat of the plains. Today's visitors to Dehra prefer to live near the markets and cinemas and many of the old houses, set amidst oak and maple and deodar, are inhabited by wild cats, bandicoots, owls, goats, and the occasional charcoal-burner or mule-driver.

But amongst these neglected mansions stood a neat, whitewashed cottage called Mulberry Lodge. And in it lived an elderly English spinster named Miss Mackenzie.

In years, Miss Mackenzie was more than 'elderly', being well over eighty. But no one would have guessed it. She was clean, sprightly, and wore old-fashioned but well-preserved dresses. Once a week, she walked the two miles to town to buy butter and jam and soap and sometimes a small bottle of eau de cologne.

She had lived in the hill station since she had been a girl in her teens, and that had been before the First World War. Though she had never married, she had experienced a few love affairs and was far from being the typical frustrated spinster of fiction. Her parents had been dead thirty years; her brother and sister were also dead. She had no relatives in India, and she lived on a small pension of forty rupees a month and the gift parcels that were sent out to her from New Zealand by a friend of her youth.

Like other lonely old people, she kept a pet, a large black cat with bright yellow eyes. In her small garden she grew dahlias, chrysanthemums, gladioli and a few rare orchids. She knew a great deal about plants, and about wild flowers, trees, birds and insects. She had never made a serious study of these things, but having lived with them for so many years, had developed an intimacy with all that grew and flourished around her.

She had few visitors. Occasionally, the padre from the local church called on her, and once a month the postman came with a letter from New Zealand or her pension papers. The milkman called every second day with a litre of

milk for the lady and her cat. And sometimes she received a couple of eggs free, for the egg-seller remembered a time when Miss Mackenzie, in her earlier prosperity, bought eggs from him in large quantities. He was a sentimental man. He remembered her as a ravishing beauty in her twenties when he had gazed at her in round-eyed, nine-year-old wonder and consternation.

Now it was September and the rains were nearly over and Miss Mackenzie's chrysanthemums were coming into their own. She hoped the coming winter wouldn't be too severe because she found it increasingly difficult to bear the cold.

One day, as she was pottering about in her garden, she saw a schoolboy plucking wild flowers on the slope about the cottage.

'Who's that?' she called. 'What are you up to, young man?'

I was alarmed and tried to dash up the hillside, but slipped on pine needles and came slithering down the slope into Miss Mackenzie's nasturtium bed.

When I found there was no escape, I gave her a bright disarming smile and said, 'Good morning, Miss.'

I was supposed to be attending my classes at the local English-medium school, so I was in my school uniform—a bright red blazer and a red and black striped tie.

'Good morning,' said Miss Mackenzie severely. 'Would you mind moving out of my flower bed?'

I stepped gingerly over the nasturtiums and looked up at Miss Mackenzie with my dimpled cheeks and appealing eyes. I was sure the lady would find it impossible to be angry with me.

'You're trespassing,' said Miss Mackenzie.

'Yes, Miss.'

'And you ought to be in school at this hour.'

'Yes, Miss.'

'Then what are you doing here?'

'Picking flowers, Miss.' And I held up a bunch of ferns and wild flowers.

'Oh.' Miss Mackenzie was finally disarmed. Perhaps it was a long time since she had seen a boy taking an interest in flowers, and, what was more, playing truant from school in order to gather them.

'Do you like flowers?' she asked.

'Yes, Miss. I'm going to be a botan—a botantist?'

'You mean a botanist.'

'Yes, Miss.'

'Well, that's unusual. Most boys at your age want to be pilots or soldiers or perhaps engineers. But you want to be a botanist. Well, well. There's still hope for the world, I see. And do you know the names of these flowers?'

'This is a bukhilo flower,' I said, showing her a small golden flower. 'That's a Pahari name. It means *puja*, or prayer. The flower is offered during prayers. But I don't know what this is . . .'

I held out a pale pink flower with a soft, heart-shaped leaf.

'It's a wild begonia,' said Miss Mackenzie. 'And that purple stuff is salvia, but it isn't wild. It's a plant that escaped from my garden. Don't you have any books on flowers?'

'No, Miss.'

'All right, come in and I'll show you a book.'

She led me into a small front room which was crowded with furniture and books and vases and jam jars, and offered me a chair. I sat awkwardly on its edge. The black cat immediately leapt on to my knees, and settled down there, purring loudly.

'What's your name?' asked Miss Mackenzie, as she rummaged among her books.

'Rusty, Miss.'

'And where do you live?'

'I live with my guardian here—in Dehra.'

'Oh, and what's that?' she asked, pointing at my blazer's pocket which was bulging.

'Bulbs, Miss.'

'Flower bulbs?'

'No, electric bulbs.'

'Electric bulbs! You might send me a few, when you get home. Mine are always fusing, and they're so expensive, like everything else these days. Ah, here we are!' She pulled a heavy volume down from the shelf and laid it on the table. '*Flora Himaliensis*, published in 1892, and probably the only copy in India. This is a very valuable book, Rusty. No other naturalist has recorded so many wild Himalayan flowers. And let me tell you this: there are many flowers and plants which are still unknown to the fancy botanists who spend all their time with microscopes instead of in the mountains. But perhaps, *you'll* do something about that, one day.'

'Yes, Miss.'

We went through the book together, and Miss Mackenzie pointed out many flowers that grew in and around the hill station, while I made notes of their names and seasons. She lit a stove, and put the kettle on for tea. And then the old lady and I sat side by side over cups of hot sweet tea, absorbed in that book of wild flowers.

'May I come again?' I asked as I rose to go.

'If you like,' said Miss Mackenzie. 'But not during school hours. You mustn't miss your classes.'

After that, I visited Miss Mackenzie about once a week, and nearly always brought a wildflower for her to identify. I knew that she looked forward to these visits but sometimes, more than a week would pass without a visit from me if I got busy with schoolwork.

Then later she'd tell me about how disappointed and lonely she had felt, and how much she had grumbled at her poor black cat.

She often said that I reminded her of her brother, when the latter had been a boy. There was the physical resemblance of course, but there was something else too. It was my eagerness, my alert bright look and the way I stood—legs apart, hands on hips, a picture of confidence—that reminded her of Andrew.

And why did I visit her so often?

Partly because she knew about wild flowers, and I really did want to become a botanist then. And partly because she smelt of freshly-baked bread, and that was a smell my grandmother had possessed. Partly because I was a little different from other children. And partly because she was lonely and sometimes a boy of twelve can sense loneliness better than an adult. There was really no one I could talk to or share my interests with at my guardian's house. I was left to my own devices and any discussion with my guardian pertained to my schooling and was dealt with cursorily.

By the middle of October, when there was only a

fortnight left for the school to close, the first snow had fallen on the distant mountains. One peak stood high above the rest, a white pinnacle against the azure-blue sky. When the sun set, this peak turned from orange to gold to pink to red.

'How high is that mountain?' I asked.

'It must be over 12,000 feet,' said Miss Mackenzie. 'About thirty miles from here, as the crow flies. I always wanted to go there, but there was no proper road. At that height, there'll be flowers that you don't get here—the blue gentian and the purple columbine, the anemone and the edelweiss.'

'I'll go there one day,' I promised myself aloud.

'I'm sure you will, if you really want to.'

The day before school closed, I went to say goodbye to Miss Mackenzie. I was to leave for Delhi two days later with my guardian who had some business to attend to there.

'I don't suppose you'll be able to find many wild flowers in Delhi,' she said. 'But have a good holiday.'

'Thank you, Miss.'

Just as I was about to leave, Miss Mackenzie, on an impulse, thrust the *Flora Himaliensis* into my hands.

'You keep it,' she said. 'It's a present for you.'

'But I'll be back soon, and I'll be able to look at it then. It's so valuable.'

'I know it's valuable and that's why I've given it to you. Otherwise it might fall into the hands of the junk dealers.'

'But, Miss . . .'

'Don't argue. Besides, I may not be here when you come back.'

'Are you going away?'

'I'm not sure. I may go to England.'

I knew that she had no intention of going to England; she had not seen the country since she was a child, and she knew she would not fit in with the life of post-war Britain. Her home was in these hills, among the oaks and maples and deodars. It was lonely, but at her age it would be lonely anywhere.

I tucked the book under my arm, straightened my tie, stood stiffly to attention and said, 'Goodbye, Miss Mackenzie.'

It was the first time that I had addressed her by her name.

When I returned several months later, the cottage wore an empty, forlorn look. Miss Mackenzie's neighbour Major Warwick told me what had happened.

Winter had set in early, and strong winds brought rain and sleet, and soon there were no flowers in the garden or on the hillside. The cat stayed indoors, curled up at the foot of Miss Mackenzie's bed.

Miss Mackenzie wrapped herself up in all her old shawls and mufflers, but still she felt the cold. Her fingers grew so stiff that she took almost an hour to open a can of baked beans. And then it snowed and for several days the milkman did not come. The postman arrived with her pension papers, but she felt too tired to take them up to town to the bank.

She spent most of the time in bed. It was the warmest place. She kept a hot-water bottle at her back, and the cat kept her feet warm. She lay in bed, dreaming of the spring and summer months. In three months' time, the primroses would be out and with the coming of spring, the local school would reopen and I was sure to be back.

One night the hot-water bottle burst and the bedding was soaked through. As there was no sun for several days, the blanket remained damp. Miss Mackenzie caught a chill and had to keep to her cold, uncomfortable bed. She knew she had a fever but there was no thermometer with which to take her temperature. She had difficulty in breathing.

A strong wind sprang up one night, and the window flew open and kept banging all night. Miss Mackenzie was too weak to get up and close it, and the wind swept the rain and sleet into the room. The cat crept into the bed and snuggled close to its mistress's warm body. But towards morning that body had lost its warmth and the cat left the bed and started scratching about on the floor.

As a shaft of sunlight streamed through the open window, the milkman arrived. He poured some milk into the cat's saucer on the doorstep and the cat leapt down from the windowsill and made for the milk. The milkman called a greeting to Miss Mackenzie, but received no answer. Her window was open and he had always known her to be up before sunrise. So he put his head in at the window and called again. But Miss Mackenzie did not answer. She had gone away to the mountain where the blue gentian and purple columbine grow.

A Job Well Done

'ARE YOU GOING to cover the well?' I asked. Puran the gardener was clearing up the weeds that grew in profusion around the old, disused well. I was a great favourite of Puran's. He had been the gardener at my grandmother's house, and now he was with my mother and stepfather.

Actually, it was only by a 'multi-coincidence' that Puran was working for them. It was 1944, and the Second World War was still on. My stepfather had enrolled in the RAF, and before he left for Peshawar—where he was stationed—he left my mother and my half-brother in Dehra. At that point, my day school had closed for summer vacation and I was at a loose end because my guardian and Mrs Harrison had to rush off to Bombay to solve some business problem.

My mother invited me over to her place and asked

me to stay there with her, at least till my guardian returned. I accepted, not because I was fond of my mother, but because I had no reason to not accept.

Puran was also at a loose end as his previous employer, an elderly English lady, had just passed away. When he realized that I was at my mother's house and that she needed a gardener, he just turned up one day and offered his services. So that's how he and I came to be at my stepfather's house that summer.

On our agenda today was the old well in the middle of the garden. 'I must cover it, I suppose,' said Puran. 'That's what the Major Sahib wants. He'll be back any day and if he finds the well still uncovered he'll get into one of his raging fits and I'll be looking for yet another job!'

The 'Major Sahib' was my stepfather, Major Summerskill. A tall, hearty, back-slapping man, who liked polo and pig-sticking. He was quite unlike my father. My father had always given me books to read. When I'd first stayed with my mother and stepfather, he had said that I would become a dreamer if I read too much and had taken my books away. I had hated him since then and did not think much of my mother for marrying him.

'The boy's too soft,' I had often heard him tell my mother.

23

Now, he had been away for about two months. Before leaving, he had left strict instructions for Puran to cover up the old well.

'Too damned dangerous having an open well in the middle of the garden. My son is too small to be told not to run around in the garden and to not peep into open wells,' my stepfather had said. 'Make sure that it's completely covered by the time I get back.'

Puran was loth to cover up the old well. He said that it had been there for over fifty years, long before the house had been built. In its walls lived a colony of pigeons. Their soft cooing filled the garden with a lovely sound. And during the hot dry summer months, when taps ran dry, the well was always a dependable source of water. The *bhisti* still used it, filling his goatskin bag with the cool, clear water and sprinkling the paths around the house to keep the dust down.

Puran pleaded with my mother to let him leave the well uncovered.

'What will happen to the pigeons?' he asked.

'Oh, surely they can find another well,' said my mother. 'Do close it up soon, Puran. I don't want the Sahib to come back and find that you haven't done anything about it.'

My mother seemed just a little bit afraid of the Major. How can we be afraid of those we love? It

24

was a question that puzzled me then and puzzles me still.

The Major's absence made life pleasant. I read books, spent long hours in the banyan tree, ate buckets of mangoes and dawdled in the garden, talking to Puran and playing with Mohan—his son. My half-brother (born to my mother from her second marriage) usually stayed indoors with Mother, playing childish games with her.

Neither Puran nor I were looking forward to the Major's return. Puran had really been my father's man. His loyalty to my father probably extended to my mother as well, for it seemed to be just for her sake that he put up with my stepfather's rude and explosive nature. My mother had always appeared deceptively frail and helpless and most men, Major Summerskill included, felt protective towards her. She liked people who did things for her.

'Your father would have liked this well,' said Puran. 'Remember the well in your grandparents' backyard? Your father would often sit there in the evenings with a book in which he made drawings of birds and flowers and insects.'

I remembered those drawings and how I had managed to keep some of those drawings with me while Grandma was selling off the house. I also remembered how some of them had been thrown away by the Major when he had chanced upon them. Puran too knew about it. I didn't keep much from him.

'It's a sad business closing this well,' said Puran again. 'Only a fool or a drunkard is likely to fall into it. Any child, however small, is unlikely to fall into it, if he is told that such a well exists.'

Nevertheless, he made his preparations. Planks of sal wood, bricks and cement were neatly piled up around the well.

'Tomorrow,' said Puran, trying to evade this unpleasant task which had been thrust upon him. 'Tomorrow I will do it. Not today. Let the birds remain for one more day. In the morning, baba, you can help me drive the birds from the well.'

On the day my stepfather was expected back, my mother hired a tonga and went to the bazaar to do some shopping. As the Major was not expected before evening, I decided to make full use of my last free morning. I took all my favourite books and stored them away in an outhouse where I could come for them from time to time. Then, my pockets bursting with mangoes, I climbed into the banyan tree. It was the darkest and coolest place on a hot day in June. From behind the screen of leaves that concealed me, I could see Puran moving about near the well. He appeared to be most unwilling to get on with the job of covering it up.

'Baba!' he called several times. But I did not feel like stirring from the banyan tree. Puran grasped a long plank of wood and placed it across one end of the well. He started hammering. From my vantage point in the banyan tree, he looked very bent and old.

A jingle of tonga bells and the squeak of unoiled wheels told me that a tonga was coming in at the gate. It was too early for my mother to be back. I peered through the thick, waxy leaves of the tree and nearly fell off my branch in surprise. It was my stepfather, the Major! He had arrived earlier than expected.

I did not come down from the tree. I had no intention of facing my stepfather until my mother returned.

The Major had climbed down from the tonga and was watching his luggage being carried on to the veranda. He was red in the face and the ends of his handlebar moustache were stiff with brilliantine. Puran approached with a half-hearted salaam.

'Ah, so there you are, you old scoundrel!' exclaimed the Major, trying to sound friendly and jocular. 'More jungle than garden, from what I can see. You're getting too old for this sort of work, fellow. Time to retire! And where's the memsahib?'

'Gone to the bazaar,' said Puran.

'And the boy?'

Puran shrugged. 'I have not seen the boy today, Sahib.'

'Damn!' said the Major. 'A fine homecoming, this. Well, wake up the cook-boy and tell him to get some sodas.'

'Cook-boy's gone away,' said Puran.

'Well, I'll be double-damned,' said the Major.

The tonga went away and the Major started pacing up and down the garden path. Then he saw Puran's unfinished work at the well. He grew purple in the face, strode across to the well, and started ranting at the old gardener.

Puran began making excuses. He said something about a shortage of bricks, the sickness of a niece, unsatisfactory cement, unfavourable weather, unfavourable gods. When none of this seemed to satisfy the Major, Puran began mumbling about something bubbling up from the bottom of the well and pointed down into its depths. The Major stepped on to the low parapet and looked down. Puran kept pointing. The Major leant over a little more.

Puran's hand moved swiftly, like a conjurer making a pass. He did not actually push the Major. He appeared merely to tap him once on the bottom. I caught a glimpse of my stepfather's boots as he disappeared into the well. I couldn't help thinking of *Alice in Wonderland*, of Alice disappearing down the rabbit hole.

There was a tremendous splash and the pigeons

flew up, circling the well thrice before settling on the roof of the bungalow.

By lunchtime—or tiffin, as we called it then—Puran had the well covered over with the wooden planks.

'The Major will be pleased,' said my mother when she came home. 'It will be quite ready by evening, won't it, Puran?' By evening the well had been completely bricked over. It was the fastest bit of work Puran had ever done.

Over the next fortnight, my mother's concern changed to anxiety, her anxiety to melancholy, and her melancholy to resignation. By being gay and high-spirited myself, I hope I did something to cheer her up. She had written to the Colonel of the Regiment and had been informed that the Major had gone home on leave several weeks ago. Somewhere, in the vastness of India, the Major had disappeared.

It was easy enough to disappear and never be found. After seven months had passed without the Major turning up, it was presumed that one of two things must have happened. Either he had been murdered on the train and his corpse flung into a river. Or, he had run away with a tribal girl and was living in some remote corner of the country.

Life had to carry on for the rest of us. The rains were over and the guava season was approaching.

My mother was receiving visits from a colonel of His Majesty's 32nd Foot. He was an elderly, easy-going, seemingly absent-minded man, who didn't get in the way at all but left slabs of chocolate lying around the house.

'A good sahib,' observed Puran as I stood beside him behind the bougainvillaea, watching the colonel saunter up the veranda steps. 'See how well he wears his sola topi! It covers his head completely.'

'He's bald underneath,' I said.

'No matter. I think he will be all right.'

'And if he isn't,' I said, 'we can always open up the well again.'

Puran dropped the nozzle of the hose pipe and water gushed out over our feet. But he recovered quickly and taking me by the hand led me across to the old well now surmounted by a three-tiered cement platform which looked rather like a wedding cake.

'We must not forget this old well,' he said. 'Let us make it beautiful, baba. Some flowerpots, perhaps.'

And together we fetched pots and decorated the covered well with ferns and geraniums. Everyone congratulated Puran on the fine job he had done. My only regret was that the pigeons had gone away.

The Woman on
Platform No. 8

IT WAS MY first year at boarding school, and I was sitting on platform no. 8 at Ambala station, waiting for the northern-bound train. I think I was about fourteen at the time. My guardian was having to go out of Dehra quite often now for business reasons. And my mother had married the colonel and left Dehra with him. There was no one to look after me in Dehra. So I was made to leave the day school I went to in Dehra and join Arundel—a boarding school at my guardian's place in Paharganj. Now after a brief vacation, I was travelling from Dehra to Kalka via Ambala. From Kalka I had to board a bus to Paharganj. Most of the time I had been pacing up and down the platform, browsing at the bookstall, or feeding broken biscuits to stray dogs; trains came and went, and the platform would be quiet for a while and then, when a train arrived, it would be an inferno of heaving, shouting, agitated human bodies. As the carriage doors opened, a tide of people would sweep down upon the nervous little ticket-collector at the gate; and every time this happened I would be caught in the rush and swept outside the station. Now tired of this game and of ambling about the platform, I sat down on my suitcase and gazed dismally across the railway tracks.

Trolleys rolled past me, and I was conscious of the cries of the various vendors—the men who sold curds and lemon, the sweetmeat-seller, the newspaper boy—but I had lost interest in all that went on along the busy platform, and continued to stare across the railway tracks, feeling bored and a little lonely.

'Are you all alone, my son?' asked a soft voice close behind me.

I looked up and saw a woman standing near me. She was leaning over, and I saw a pale face and dark, kind eyes. She wore no jewels, and was dressed very simply in a white sari.

'Yes, I am going to school,' I said, and stood up respectfully.

She seemed poor, but there was a dignity about her that commanded respect.

'I have been watching you for some time,' she said. 'Didn't your parents come to see you off?'

'I don't live here,' I said. 'I had to change trains. Anyway, I can travel alone.'

'I am sure you can,' she said, and I liked her for saying that, and I also liked her for the simplicity of her dress, and for her deep, soft voice and the serenity of her face.

'Tell me, what is your name?' she asked.

'Rusty,' I said.

'And how long do you have to wait for your train?'

'About an hour, I think. It comes at twelve o'clock.'

'Then come with me and have something to eat.'

I was going to refuse, out of shyness and suspicion, but she took me by the hand, and then I felt it would be silly to pull my hand away. She told a coolie to look after my suitcase, and then she led me away down the platform. Her hand was gentle, and she held mine neither too firmly nor too lightly. I looked up at her again. She was not young. And she was not old. She must have been over thirty, but had she been fifty, I think she would have looked much the same.

She took me into the station dining room, ordered tea and samosas and jalebis, and at once I began to thaw and take a new interest in this kind woman. Our strange encounter had little effect on my appetite. I was a hungry schoolboy, and I ate as much as I could in as polite a manner as possible. She took obvious pleasure in watching me eat, and I think it was the food that strengthened the bond between us and cemented our friendship, for under the influence of the tea and sweets I began to talk quite freely, and told her about my school, my friends, my likes and dislikes. She questioned me quietly from time to time, but preferred listening; she drew me out very well, and I soon forgot that we were strangers. But she did not ask me about my family or where I lived, and I did not ask her where she lived. I accepted her for what she had been to me—a quiet, kind and gentle woman who gave sweets to a lonely boy on a railway platform . . .

After about half an hour we left the dining room and began walking back along the platform. An engine was shunting up and down beside platform no. 8, and as it approached, a boy leapt off the platform and ran across the rails, taking a shortcut to the next platform. He was at a safe distance from the engine, but as he leapt across the rails, the woman clutched my arm. Her fingers dug into my flesh, and I winced with pain. I caught her fingers and looked up at her, and I saw a spasm of pain and fear and sadness pass across her face. She watched the boy as he climbed the platform, and it was not until he had disappeared in the crowd that she relaxed her hold on my arm. She smiled at me reassuringly, and took my hand again, but her fingers trembled against mine.

'He was all right,' I said, feeling that it was she who needed reassurance.

She smiled gratefully at me and pressed my hand. We walked together in silence until we reached the place where I had left my suitcase. One of my schoolfellows, Satish, had turned up with his mother.

'Hello, Rusty!' he called. 'The train's coming in late, as usual. Did you know we have a new headmaster this year?' We shook hands, and then he turned to his mother and said, 'This is Rusty, Mother. He is one of my friends, and the best student in the class.'

'I am glad to know that,' said his mother, a large, imposing woman who wore spectacles. She looked at the woman who held my hand and said, 'And I suppose you're Rusty's mother?'

I opened my mouth to make some explanation, but before I could say anything the woman replied, 'Yes, I am Rusty's mother.' I was unable to speak a word. I looked quickly up at the woman, but she did not appear to be at all embarrassed, and was smiling at Satish's mother.

Satish's mother said, 'It's such a nuisance having to wait for the train right in the middle of the night. But one can't let the child wait here alone. Anything can happen to a boy at a big station like this—there are so many suspicious characters hanging about. These days one has to be very careful of strangers.'

'Rusty can travel alone though,' said the woman beside me, and somehow I felt grateful to her for saying that. I had already forgiven her for lying; besides, I had taken an instinctive dislike to Satish's mother.

'Well, be very careful, Rusty,' cautioned Satish's mother looking sternly at me through her spectacles. 'Be very careful when your mother is not with you. And never talk to strangers!' I looked at Satish's mother and then looked at the woman who had given me tea and sweets, and looked back at Satish's mother.

'I like strangers,' I said.

Satish's mother definitely staggered a little, as she was obviously not used to being contradicted by anyone, especially youngsters. 'There you are, you see! If you don't watch over them all the time, they'll walk straight into trouble. Always listen to what your mother tells you,' she said, wagging a fat little finger at me. 'And never, never talk to strangers.'

I glared resentfully at her, and moved closer to the woman who had befriended me. Satish was standing behind his mother, grinning at me, and delighting in my clash with his mother. Apparently he was on my side.

The station bell clanged, and the people who had till now been squatting resignedly on the platform began bustling about.

'Here it comes!' shouted Satish, as the engine whistle shrieked and its front lights played over the rails.

The train moved slowly into the station, the engine hissing and sending out waves of steam. As it came to a stop, Satish jumped on to the footboard of a lighted compartment and shouted, 'Come on, Rusty, this one's empty!' and I picked up my suitcase and made a dash for the open door.

We placed ourselves at the open windows, and the two women stood outside on the platform, talking up to us. Satish's mother did most of the talking.

'Now don't jump on and off moving trains, as you did just now,' she said. 'And don't stick your heads out of the windows, and don't eat any rubbish on the way.' She allowed me to share the benefit of her advice, as she probably didn't think my 'mother' a very capable person. She handed Satish a bag of fruit, a cricket bat and a big box of chocolates, and told him to share the food with me. Then she stood back from the window to watch how my 'mother' behaved.

I was smarting under the patronizing tone of Satish's mother, who obviously thought mine a very poor family; and I did not intend giving the other woman away. I let her take my hand in hers, but I could think of nothing to say. I was conscious of Satish's mother staring at us with hard, beady eyes, and I found myself hating her with a firm, unreasoning hate. The guard walked up the platform, blowing his whistle for the train to leave. I looked straight into the eyes of the woman who held my hand, and she smiled in a gentle, understanding way. I leaned out of the window then, and put my lips to her cheek, and kissed her.

The carriage jolted forward, and she drew her hand away.

'Good-bye, Mother!' shouted Satish, as the train began to move slowly out of the station. Satish and his mother waved to each other.

'Good-bye,' I said to the other woman, 'good-bye—Mother.'

I didn't wave or shout, but sat still in front of the window, gazing at the woman on the platform. Satish's mother was talking to her, but she didn't appear to be listening; she was looking at me, as the train took me away. She stood there on the busy platform, a pale sweet woman in white, and I watched her until she was lost in the milling crowd.

Running Away

AS THE BIG clock on the top of the school pavilion struck eleven, I crept out of bed, slipped on my gym shoes, and moved silently across the dormitory.

I stopped in the doorway and peered back into the dark room to make sure that no one else was awake, then I hurried along the corridor and down the stairs.

Daljit was already on the veranda. He was a Sikh and a good friend of mine—we studied in the same class. He had removed his turban for the night and his long hair was now bunched up on his head in a big knot. The white pyjama-suit he was wearing stood out like a beacon in the darkness. If any teachers were about, we would certainly be seen.

Daljit put a finger to his lips as soon as he saw me. This was quite unnecessary, since I was the cautious one, but Daljit was enjoying himself, and wanted to make everything seem mysterious.

Tiptoeing was not in Daljit's line; he had big feet, and was often teased about them. There is a saying in Punjab that if you have big feet you will be good only for manual work. Daljit denied this. Instead, he said that if you had big feet you would travel a lot, and he was now out to prove his theory.

We ran silently across the flat in front of the pavilion, while heavy monsoon clouds scurried overhead. Running down the pavilion steps, we entered the gymnasium. The gym door was usually left open, and it was in this huge damp room, smelling of coir-matting, varnish and perspiration, that we held our nocturnal meetings.

This was to be our final meeting before running away from school.

'Have you got everything ready?' asked Daljit, lighting a candle stub and placing it on the floor between us.

We sat cross-legged, facing each other. The candle cast a glow on Daljit's round, good-natured face. It left me in the shadows.

'Yes. Everything's ready,' I replied. 'A knife, two packets of biscuits, some bread, a tin of sardines, and some sweets.'

The bread, which had been pocketed during the previous week's meals, was now quite stale and hard, but I wanted to make my list as long as possible.

'Not much,' commented Daljit. 'And how much money do you have?'

'Six rupees. That's two months' pocket money.'

'Not bad, Rusty.' He knew I did not get much pocket money from my guardian. 'Well, I've got about thirty rupees, so we don't have to worry too much about money—not yet, anyway. And I've got some cheese, jam, chocolate and pickle which I saved from my last parcel.'

'Pickle with chocolate?'

'No, of course not. But it will go with any stuff we'll get to eat on the way.'

Daljit frequently received food parcels from his father who was a businessman in East Africa. Part of Daljit's plan was to get back to Africa because he was fed up with living in a boarding school in India. This was where we joined forces. My uncle Jim was the captain of a small tramp-steamer which sometimes plied between Mombasa in East Africa and either Jamnagar or Dwarka, two small ports on the west coast of India. His ship, the O.H. *Iris*, was due to call at Jamnagar at the end of the month, and we hoped to persuade him to take us on board.

Daljit wanted to get back to Africa. He was certain his father would realize that if he could get back to Africa on his own from India, it might not be a good idea after all to send him to school in India once again.

I too wanted to get away—but for different reasons. True, school was one of them. Though not as grim as Dickens's Dotheboy's Hall, it was not a good school. The principal ran the place more as a business enterprise than as a school. 'Give a little, take a lot,' was his motto. He charged his fees, and in return gave us bad teachers and worse food. At any rate, that's what we boys thought.

Daljit, of course, had only himself to blame for ending up in Arundel. He had refused to settle down in any of the other schools he had been sent to, and had, by a process of elimination, come to Arundel, where, after only three months of a diet consisting mostly of lentil soup and mutton fat, he was eager to get away.

'I'll have no more schools after this one,' he declared. 'I'll go straight into my father's business in Nairobi. I can read and write, and I know the difference between a profit and a loss. That's all I need. What about you, Rusty?'

'I want to be a writer,' I said. Gone were the days when I wanted to study plants and become a botanist. I was now fifteen years old. Big enough to make up my mind for once and for all. 'I don't mind going to a school, but I have been here for a year now, and I don't like it one bit, and I know my guardian won't send me to any other.'

Mr Harrison had sent me to Arundel because the principal was a friend of his, and he had only to pay half-fees for me. Before coming to Arundel, I had attended a day school and stayed with my guardian and his wife. But they travelled often for business purposes and I think they found it very irksome to look after me as I grew older. I was inclined to be rebellious, to spend my time in the bazaars instead of at home, and to read books instead of taking an interest in manly pastimes like those enjoyed by my guardian, which consisted of shooting wild animals. I had never cared much for my guardian and he had been disappointed in me.

But the main reason for running away was not to get back to the bazaars or my guardian's house, but to reach my uncle's ship in Jamnagar.

Uncle Jim was another of my father's cousins. He had last seen me when I was a small boy of five and had written to me off and on throughout the years. His letters had been gay and came in envelopes that bore colourful stamps of different countries. They came from Valparaiso, San Diego, San Francisco, Buenos Aires, Dar-es-Salaam, Mombasa, Freetown, Singapore, Bombay, Marseilles, London . . . these were some of the places where Uncle Jim's ship called. He was seldom on the same route, and seemed to move leisurely across the oceans of the earth, calling at ports which had only the most romantic associations for me, for I had already read Stevenson, Captain Marryat, some Conrad and W.W. Jacobs.

In his letters, Uncle Jim often spoke of my joining him at sea—'When you are a little older, Rusty.'

I felt I was old enough now. I was sick of school and sick of my guardian. But that was not all. I was in love with the world. I wanted to see the world, every corner of it, the places I had read about in books—the junks and sampans of Hong Kong, the palm-fringed lagoons of the Indies, the streets of London, the beautiful ebony-skinned people of Africa, the bright birds and exotic plants of the Amazon . . .

When Uncle Jim's last letter had arrived, telling me that his ship would call at Jamnagar towards the end of the month, I felt a deep thrill of anticipation. Here was my chance at last! True, Uncle Jim had said nothing about my joining him, but he was not to know that I was seriously considering it.

It was not simply a question of walking out of school and taking a quick ride down to the docks. Jamnagar, on the west coast, was at least 800 miles from Paharganj, the hill station in northern India where Arundel was located. Eight hundred miles!

I doubt if I would have made the attempt if Daljit had not agreed to come too. It isn't much fun running away on your own. It is even worse if you have a companion who is full of enthusiasm at the beginning and who backs out at the last moment. This leaves one feeling defeated and crushed.

Daljit was not that kind of companion. He meant the things he said. About a month earlier, when I had told him of my uncle's ship and my wish to get to it, he had said, without a moment's hesitation: 'I'm coming too!'

Daljit lived impulsively. Sometimes he made mistakes. But he never went halfway and stopped. Someone had to stop him, otherwise he did whatever it was he set out to do.

We had become friends during the early monsoon marathon runs. I was much better at short races, and Daljit was a little too chubby to keep up with the other boys. Allowing the good athletes to forge ahead, I would sit down on a grassy knoll and read a comic or a chapter from *David Copperfield*. One evening, while I was making use of the run in this way, I saw Daljit strolling down the road, whistling cheerfully.

'Aren't you in the race?' I asked.

'Yes. Aren't you?'

'Yes,' I said, and returned to my book.

Daljit sat down beside me.

'They won't miss us if we're a little late,' he said. 'Why don't we go over to that stall and eat some hot *pakoras*? Don't worry about money. I have more than enough. I can't stop my mother from spoiling me.'

It was the beginning of a steady friendship. Based initially on *pakoras*, and a mutual aversion to long-distance races, it soon developed a stronger foundation. After several marathons together, we felt we had known each other for years.

Now, sitting together in the dark, high-ceilinged gymnasium, we felt we understood each other perfectly. I did not mind the fact that Daljit had more money. He did not mind the fact that I was more 'brainy', as he put it. He was impressed by the extent of my reading. But I was an impractical fellow, and in the ways of the world Daljit was more experienced.

He pulled a folder from his pyjama-suit and opened it out on the floor. It was a railway map of India. We had purchased it during our last and final marathon run, a memorable occasion when we had cut off to the bazaar, and then, having made several purchases, taken a shortcut back to school, arriving first and second respectively in the race. (We were, of course, disqualified when the judges came back and insisted that they had not seen us anywhere along the prescribed route,

48

but we had our few moments of glory, with everyone congratulating us on our victory.)

With the map spread out before us, I took a red pencil and circled Paharganj in the Himalayan foothills. Then I circled Jamnagar, at the tip of the Kathiawar Peninsula, facing the Gulf of Kutch. What lay in between? First, hills and forests; then the flat, fertile plains of the Doab (the Ganga-Jamuna basin) stretching to a little beyond Delhi; then the bare brown hills and sand dunes of the Rajasthan desert; and finally the fertile coastal regions of Gujarat and Maharashtra. There were rivers and lakes. We would make what use we could of all available means of transport, as we did not have much time to lose. Uncle Jim's ship would not stay in port any longer than was necessary; it would sail again at the end of July, before the monsoon became too troublesome.

'We must get to Delhi as soon as possible,' I pointed out, 'otherwise we'll be caught easily. Once Delhi has been left behind, they won't know where to look. India's too big. It's easy to get lost.'

'Do you think they'd bother to look for us?'

'Yes, of course. Remember, my guardian is a friend of the principal. And your father will sue the school if anything happens to you. As soon as they find us missing, they'll start searching in Paharganj, and if they don't find us here or in Dehra, they'll inform the police, and we'll be on the Wanted list, like criminals. The railway stations and bus stands will be watched.'

'Does that mean we're going to *walk* to Delhi?' asked Daljit, looking dismayed. 'I can't walk 200 miles.'

'We'll walk only as far as Dehra. That's twenty miles, downhill. Can you manage that?'

'I suppose so, if it's all downhill.'

'From Dehra we'll have to get a train or a bus or a truck. We'll have to avoid the railway stations.'

'All right, Rusty. That's fine. Let's not plan too far ahead. Let's get to Delhi first. It's far enough. After that, we'll take our chances.'

We fell silent for a few minutes, busy with our own thoughts—thinking of the consequences if we were caught, of the dangers and difficulties we might encounter. The candle spluttered and went out. There was total darkness for a minute, then a thin light darted across the floor and over my feet.

'Do you like my pencil torch?' asked Daljit. 'Made in Japan, and designed by James Bond. I bought it in Nairobi last year. But we mustn't waste the battery; this size isn't available here.' He switched it off.

'You must have been terribly spoilt at home,' I said enviously. At times I felt that it was unfair that some children should enjoy being indulged by their family so much when I didn't even have a family to my name anymore.

'I was,' said Daljit with a chuckle. 'In fact, I'm still thoroughly spoilt!' He gave me his hand. 'It's tomorrow night, then?' he whispered. There was no need to whisper, but Daljit never let up a chance to dramatize things.

'Yes, tomorrow night,' I said.

'Where do we meet?'

'Down in the pine forest. Near the big rock. At ten. From there we'll follow the stream until we meet the bridle-path to Dehra.'

'Be on time,' said Daljit. 'I don't want to be waiting for you in the dark, in the middle of the forest. They say it's haunted.'

'Well, you have your torch,' I said reassuringly.

He gripped my hand again. 'We won't talk to each other in school tomorrow. No one must have any suspicion. Now let's go to bed, I'm sleepy.'

'Sleep well,' I said. 'There won't be much sleep for us from tomorrow.'

As we emerged from the gymnasium, we saw that the moon had risen. The flat, the pavilion and the dormitory building stood out clearly in the moonlight. The deodars threw ghostly shadows on the hillside. There were only a few clouds drifting overhead. It was a beautiful night.

'I hope we don't get spotted,' said Daljit.

51

'If you're caught, say you saw me sleepwalking, and followed to keep an eye on me.'

'That's a good idea. I suppose you get your brilliant ideas out of books.'

We flitted across the flat like a couple of ghouls, and ran swiftly upstairs to our dormitories.

At the entrance to his dormitory, Daljit turned and gave me a conspiratorial wave. I crept into my bed and tried to sleep. But sleep was elusive. I kept thinking of our coming adventure, imagining the kind of journey we would have, and visualizing my uncle's surprise when we turned up on his ship.

I would work for my passage, of course. Daljit and I could be deckhands.

Yokohama, Valparaiso, San Diego, London!

Running away from school! It is not to be recommended to everyone. Parents and teachers would disapprove. Or would they, deep down in their hearts? Everyone has wanted to run away, at some time in his life, if not from a bad school or an unhappy home, then from something equally unpleasant. Running away seems to be in the best of traditions. Huck Finn did it. So did Master Copperfield and Oliver Twist. So did Kim. Various enterprising young men have run away to sea. Most great men have run away from school at some stage in their lives; and if they haven't, then perhaps it is something they should have done. Anyway, Daljit and I ran away from school, and we did it quite successfully too, up to a point. But then, all this happened in India, which, though it forms only two per cent of the world's land mass, has fifteen per cent of its population, and so it is an easy place to hide in, or be lost in, or disappear in, and never be seen or heard of again!

Not that we intended disappearing. We were headed for a particular place—Jamnagar—and as soon as I took my first step into the unknown, that first step on the slippery pine needles below the school, I knew quite definitely that I wasn't running away from anything, but that I was running *towards* something. Call it a dream, if you like. I was running towards a dream.

In bare feet and pyjamas, I slid down the steep slope of the hill, and was the first to reach the flat rock in the middle of the forest. There was a soft breeze sighing in the pine trees. The night was pleasant and cool. From the ravine below came the subdued murmur of the stream; it made a sound like a man humming rather tunelessly to himself. The full moon came out from behind massed monsoon clouds, and the trees, bushes and boulders emerged from the darkness.

Daljit arrived a few minutes later. Though still in his pyjamas, he was wearing his turban. Daljit's turban was a source of great pride to him as turbans are to most Sikhs. He removed it only at night, or for games, and he would never have dreamt of running away bareheaded. When going to bed that night he had taken it off without unwinding it, and on leaving bed he had put it on again like a hat, very neatly, without spoiling a single fold.

We had brought our gym clothes along in bundles and changed into them before going any further as our school clothes would be too conspicuous and our home clothes were packed away in the box room during the term. We had put on our gym shoes. Our haversacks were filled with our provisions; pyjamas, and a couple of books, went in with them. The bulk of our possessions—our clothes, bedding and boxes—we had gaily left behind.

A narrow path ran downhill, and we followed it until it levelled out, running parallel with the small stream that rumbled down the mountainside. We followed the stream for a mile, walking swiftly and silently, until we met the bridle path which was little more than a mule track going steeply down the last hills to the valley.

The going was easy. We knew the road well. And by

the time we reached the last foothills it was beginning to rain, not heavily, but as a light, thin drizzle.

We took shelter in a small dhaba on the outskirts of a village. The dhabawallah was sleeping, and his dog, a mangy pariah with only one ear, sniffed at us in a friendly way instead of chasing us off the premises.

We sat down on an old bench and watched the sun rising over the distant mountains.

This was something I have always remembered. Not because it was a more beautiful sunrise than on any other day, but because the special importance of that morning made me look at everything in a new way, hence the details still stand out clearly in my memory.

As the sky grew lighter, the pines and deodars stood out clearly, and the birds came to life. A black-bird started it all with a low, mellow call, and then the thrushes began chattering in the bushes. A barbet shrieked monotonously at the top of a spruce tree, and as the sky grew lighter still, a flock of bright green parrots flew low over the trees.

The drizzle continued and there was a bright crimson glow in the east. And then, quite suddenly, the sun shot through a gap in the clouds, and the lush green monsoon grass sprang into relief. Both Daljit and I were wonderstruck. Never before had we been up so early. Hundreds of spiderwebs, which were spun in trees and bushes and on the grass, where they would not normally have been noticed, were now clearly visible, spangled with gold and silver raindrops. The strong silk threads of the webs held the light rain and the sun, making each drop of water look like a tiny jewel.

A great wild dahlia, its scarlet flowers drenched and heavy, sprawled over the hillside and an emerald-green grasshopper reclined on a petal, stretching its legs in the sunshine.

The dhabawallah was now up. His dog, emboldened by his master's presence, began to bark at us. The man lit a charcoal fire in a *choolah*, and put on it a kettle of water to boil.

'Would you like to eat something?' he asked conversationally in Hindi.

'No, just tea for us,' I said.

He placed two brass tumblers on a table.

'The milk hasn't yet been delivered,' he said. 'You're very early.'

'We'll take the tea without milk,' said Daljit, 'but give us lots of sugar.'

'Sugar is costly these days. But because you are schoolboys, and need more, you can help yourselves.'

'Oh, we are not schoolboys,' I said hurriedly.

'Not at all,' added Daljit.

'We are just tourists,' I lied unconvincingly.

'We have to catch the early train at Dehra,' offered Daljit.

'But there's no train before ten o'clock,' said the puzzled dhabawallah.

'It is the ten o'clock train we are catching!' said Daljit smartly. 'Do you think we will be down in time?'

'Oh yes, there's plenty of time . . .'

The dhabawallah poured out steaming hot tea into the tumblers and placed the sugar bowl in front of us. 'At first I thought you were schoolboys,' he said with a laugh. 'I thought you were running away.'

Daljit almost gave us away by laughing nervously. 'What made you think that?' he asked.

'Oh, I've been here many years,' the dhabawallah replied, gesturing towards the small clearing in which his little wooden stall stood, almost like a trading outpost in a wild country. 'Schoolboys always pass this way when they're running away!'

'Do many run away?' I asked. I felt a little downcast at the thought that Daljit and I were not the first to embark on such an adventure.

'Not many. Just two or three every year. They get as far as the railway station in Dehra and there they're caught!'

'It is silly of them to get caught,' said Daljit disgustedly.

'Are they always caught?' I asked.

'Always! I give them a glass of tea on their way down, and I give them a glass of tea on their way up, when they are returning with their teachers.'

'Well, you won't be seeing *us* again,' said Daljit, ignoring the warning look that I gave him.

'Ah, but you aren't schoolboys!' said the shopkeeper, beaming at us. 'And you aren't running away!'

We paid for our tea and hurried on down the path. The parrots flew over again, screeching loudly, and settled in a lichee tree. The sun was warmer now, and as the altitude decreased, the temperature and humidity rose and we could almost smell the heat of the plains rising to meet us.

The hills levelled out into the rolling countryside, patterned with fields. Rice had been planted out, and the sugarcane was waist-high.

The path had become quite slushy. Removing our shoes and wrapping them in newspaper, we walked barefoot in the soft mud. All these little out-of-routine acts simply added to our excitement and thrill, making everything quite unforgettable for life.

'It's about three miles into Dehra,' I said. 'We must go round the town. By now, everyone in school will be up and they'll have found out we've gone!'

'We must avoid the Dehra station then,' said Daljit.

'We'll walk to the next station, Raiwala. Then we'll hop on to the first train that comes along.'

'How far must we walk?'

'About ten miles.'

'Ten miles!' Daljit looked dismayed. 'It'll take us all day!'

Well, we can't stop here nor can we wander about in Dehra, neither can we enter the station. We have to keep on walking.'

'All right, Rusty. We'll keep on walking. I suppose the beginning of an adventure is always the most difficult part.'

Already the fields were giving way to jungle. But there were still some fields of sugarcane stretching away from the railway lines.

'How much further do we have to walk?' asked Daljit impatiently. 'Is Raiwala in the middle of the jungle?'

'Yes, I think it is. We've covered about four miles I suppose. Six to go! It's funny how some miles seem longer than others. It depends on what one is thinking about, I suppose. If our thoughts are pleasant, the miles are not so long.'

'Then let's keep thinking pleasant thoughts. Isn't

there a shortcut anywhere, Rusty? You've been in these forests before.'

'We'll take the firepath through the jungle. It'll save us three or four miles. But we'll have to swim or wade across a small river. The rains have only just started, so the water shouldn't be too swift or deep.'

Heavy forests have paths cut through them at various places to prevent forest fires from spreading easily. These paths are not used much by people since they don't lead anywhere in particular, but they are frequently used by the larger animals.

We had gone about a mile along the path when we heard the sound of rushing water. The path emerged from the forest of sal trees and stopped on the banks of the small river I had mentioned earlier. The main bridge across the river stood on the main road, about three miles downstream.

'It isn't more than waist-deep anywhere,' I said. 'But the water is swift and the stones are slippery.'

We removed our clothes and tied everything into two bundles, which we carried on our heads. Daljit was a well-built boy, strong in the arms and thighs. I was slimmer. But I had quick reflexes.

The stones were quite slippery underfoot, and we stumbled, hindering rather than helping each other. We stopped in mid-stream, waist-deep, hesitating about going any further for fear of being swept off our feet.

'I can hardly stand,' said Daljit.

'It shouldn't get worse,' I said hopefully. But the current was strong, and I felt very wobbly at the knees.

Daljit tried to move forward, but slipped and went over backwards into the water, bringing me down too. He began kicking and thrashing about in fear, but eventually, using me as a support, he came up spouting water like a whale.

When we found we were not being swept away, we stopped struggling and cautiously made our way to the opposite bank, but we had been thrust about twenty yards downstream.

We rested on warm sand, while a hot sun beat down on us. Daljit sucked at a cut in his hand. But we were soon up and walking again, hungry now, and munching biscuits.

'We haven't far to go,' I said.

'I don't want to think about it,' said Daljit.

We shuffled along the forest path, tired but not discouraged.

Soon we were on the main road again, and there were fields and villages on either side. A cool breeze came across the open plain, blowing down from the hills. In the fields there was a gentle swaying movement as the wind stirred the cane. Then the breeze came down the road, and dust began to swirl and eddy around us. Out of the dust, behind us, came the rumble of cart wheels.

'Ho! Heeyah! Heeyah!' shouted the driver of the cart. The bullocks snorted and came lumbering through the dust. We moved to the side of the road.

'Are you going to Raiwala?' called Daljit. 'Can you take us with you?'

'Climb up!' said the man, and we ran through the dust and clambered on to the back of the moving cart. The cart lurched forward and rattled and bumped so much that we had to cling to its sides to avoid falling off. It smelt of grass and mint and cow-dung cakes. The driver had a red cloth tied round his head, and wore a tight vest and a dhoti. He was smoking a beedi, and yelling at his bullocks, and he seemed to have forgotten our presence. We were too busy clinging to the sides of the cart to bother about making conversation. Before long we were involved in the traffic of Raiwala—a small but busy market town. We jumped off the bullock cart and walked beside it. 'Should we offer him any money?' I asked. 'No. He will be offended. He is not a taxi driver.' 'All right, we'll just say thank you.' We called out our thanks to the cart driver, but he didn't look back. He appeared to be talking to his bullocks.

'I'm hungry,' declared Daljit. 'We haven't had a proper meal since last night.'

'Then let's eat,' I said. 'Come on, Daljit.' We walked through the small Raiwala bazaar, looking in at the tea and sweet shops until we found the cheapest-looking dhaba. A servant-boy brought us rice and dal and Daljit ordered an ounce of ghee which he poured over the curry. The meal cost us two rupees but we could have as much dal as we wanted, and between us we finished four bowls of it.

'We'll rest at the station,' I said, as we emerged from the dhaba. 'We'll buy second-class tickets, and rest in the first-class waiting room. No one will check on us. We look first class, don't we?'

'Not after that walk through the jungle,' replied Daljit.

But we did occupy the best waiting room and Daljit made himself comfortable in an armchair.

'Wake me when the train comes in,' he said drowsily.

We didn't have long to wait. I was leaning against the door, staring across the railway tracks, when I heard the whistle of the approaching train. It came in slowly, the big, hissing engine sending out waves of steam. A crowd was waiting on the platform, and it surged forward as the train drew up. At the same time the carriage doors opened and passengers started pouring out.

I had to shake Daljit to wake him up, and we emerged on to the platform to join the fray. Men, women and children pushed and struggled, and bundles of belongings were passed through windows over the heads of people. Daljit and I, clinging to our bundles, were caught up in the general rush and confusion, and were conveniently swept into a compartment.

By the time we had settled down in a corner seat, the train was moving. One or two people still hung on to the doors and windows, worming their way in as opportunity offered.

I was near a window, and as the train gathered speed and mango groves and villages mingled with telegraph posts as we rushed past, I realized that we were now really on our way, moving into the mysterious unknown. In my excitement I gripped Daljit by the arm.

'We are on our way!' I said.

'That's obvious,' said Daljit, who was trying to extract his haversack from under a fat fellow passenger who had fallen asleep on it in the midst of all the commotion.

But Daljit knew what I meant, and after retrieving the haversack, he gave me a grin, and his eyes were alive with excitement.

64

At Old Delhi Station we got down from the train like perfectly respectable people and moved confidently towards the exit, quite pleased at the prospect of handing over our tickets to the ticket-collector. The crowd was dense and movement slow. And this was a good thing, because when we were only about thirty feet from the exit, I spotted Mr Jain, our maths teacher, talking to the ticket-collector.

Mr Jain was the most efficient teacher we had at Arundel and he had obviously been sent after us. He was tubby and wore glasses, but he was a shrewd man and knew just where to intercept us. We had to get away from the exit right away.

'Let's get away from here,' I whispered fiercely, grabbing at Daljit.

'Why?' asked Daljit, who had not yet spotted our teacher.

'Can't you see?' I said. 'With the ticket-collector!'

Daljit almost tripped himself up in his hurry to vanish. The crowd was pushing towards the exit, and we were up against a human wall which would not give way at any point. Just then Mr Jain spotted us, and we heard him shout:

'Boys, come here! Rusty! Daljit!'

For a brief moment, I was on the verge of obeying the familiar voice of my teacher; and then I had a swift vision of classrooms and dormitories and the principal's gloomy, rat-whiskered face, and I hated it all and wanted to get away as fast as I could; I wanted to keep running until I reached the sea and my uncle's ship.

Daljit did not hesitate for a moment. He plunged beneath the legs of a tall Jat farmer, and almost lost his turban as he went through. I headed for a narrow gap between two stout Punjabi women, but they closed their ranks before I was completely through, and the result was a tangle of legs and arms. Mr Jain was close behind me. And then a coolie sprinted across the platform to get to a compartment, and collided with Mr Jain.

Mr Jain rolled over and lost his glasses. I disengaged myself from the women and ran after Daljit who was far ahead, using his fists and elbows to cut a path through the crowd.

He stopped once, turned to see if I had freed myself, and shouted: 'Come on, Rusty! Across the railway tracks!'

He leapt down from the platform, and slipped between two carriages of a waiting train. I followed unwillingly. I have always had a superstitious dread of crossing railway lines, and sometimes I'd get nightmares in which I'd find myself lying helpless (though not bound) on a railway track, while a steam engine thundered towards me. I'd somehow manage to get away all of a sudden in the nick of time, with the engine about three feet away, but sometimes I'd wonder what would happen if I failed to get up at the crucial moment!

Daljit had already crossed two sets of railway lines, and was climbing the railings on the other side. I looked left, and then right, and then left again, and saw a shunting engine in the distance. It was far away, and I had plenty of time in which to cross the lines and join Daljit. But I was overcome by an irrational fear and sweat broke out on my forehead and on the palms of my hands.

'Come on!' called Daljit urgently.

I took a deep breath, looked straight ahead and made a dash across the tracks. I was so nervous that I tripped and fell across the lines. A feeling of nausea swept over me and the ground seemed to be in the throes of an earthquake. Was my nightmare going to come true at last? I could still hear Daljit shouting; I could hear the puff-puff of the engine coming closer.

'Come on, Rusty, get up,' Daljit's voice was in my ear now, and I was surprised to find him beside me, tugging at my arm.

His presence gave me confidence. I scrambled to my feet, snatched up my haversack, and ran with him to the embankment. A fence made of corrugated iron sheeting blocked our way. It was about ten feet high and there were no footholds which would enable us to climb it. So we ran along the side of the fence until we found an opening which gave on to a goods yard.

We dashed through an open turnstile, and entered a small side street. We kept running, keeping to narrow lanes and alleys, where small mosques, temples, schools and shops jostled with each other, and then found ourselves on a wide thoroughfare, bustling with people and noisy with traffic.

We were in Chandni Chowk, Delhi's famed and historic street of silversmiths.

Here, in the crowd of shoppers, pedlars, clerks, urchins, sadhus, jewellers, barbers and pickpockets, we felt fairly safe. The heart of a city is always a good place to get lost in. Fugitives usually make the mistake of fleeing into the countryside, where, being strangers, they are soon noticed. By sheer accident we had come upon the safest place in Delhi.

Tongas, bullock carts, cycles, scooter-rickshaws, and cars new, old and ancient, all struggled for advantage on the road. Any vehicle that had a horn blew it and anything that had a bell jangled it, and if you had neither horn nor bell, you used your vocal chords.

We found a sweet stall, and while Daljit dropped syrupy, brown gulab jamuns down his throat, I helped myself to some golden-spangled jalebies.

A sudden sharp shower drove us into the shelter of a veranda. As it began to rain quite heavily, the street rapidly emptied, and in no time at all the throng of people had melted away. A couple of cars churned their way through the rushing water and stray cows continued rummaging in the garbage heaps.

A group of small boys came romping along the street which was now like a river in spate. When they came to a gutter filled with rainwater, they plunged in, screaming with laughter. A garland of marigolds came floating down the middle of the road.

And then the rain stopped suddenly. The sun came out. A paper boat came sailing between my legs.

'Where do we go now?' asked Daljit. 'The station isn't safe.'

'We must leave Delhi by some other way. Meanwhile, let's find a cheap hotel for the night.'

'Oh that's not a problem, I've still got over thirty rupees,' said Daljit.

'Even then, I don't think it will be enough for both of us, not if we are going to buy tickets.'

'Then we won't buy tickets,' said Daljit rather flippantly.

It didn't take us long to find a hotel. It was called the Great Oriental Hotel, and was just behind the police station. It didn't pretend to be even a third-class hotel, and for five rupees we were given a small back room which had a window overlooking the godown of an Afghan spice merchant. The powerful smell of asafoetida came up from the courtyard below.

We were tired and hot, so we tossed our belongings down on the floor and took turns at the bathroom tap. Then we stretched out on the only cot in the room and slept through the afternoon, oblivious to the noises from the street, the attentions of the insect population in the hotel mattress and the creaking of the old fan overhead.

It was late evening when we woke up, and we were hungry again. Daljit opened the door and shouted. Presently a servant-boy appeared.

'Bring us tea, toast, two big omelettes and a bottle of tomato sauce,' ordered Daljit with a confidence that I wished I had.

The omelettes, when they arrived twenty minutes later, were tiny. Both had obviously been made from one egg. The sauce had been diluted with water, and the toasts were burnt. The salt was damp, and we had to prise open the salt cellar to get to it. The pepper, however, came out in a generous rush and made up the major portion of the meal. As our hunger had not been satisfied by this poor fare, we ordered eggs again, boiled eggs this time. No matter how tiny, they would have to be whole.

'Let's go out,' said Daljit after we had eaten the eggs. 'It's stuffy in here.'

'I'm still sleepy,' I said.

'Then I'll go out for a little while. I may go to the gurdwara.'

'All right, but don't get lost.'

Daljit left me, and I settled back on the cot, and opened Tagore's *The Gardener* but I didn't read for long because as the evening wore on, I found myself a witness to the great yearly flight of the insects into the cool brief freedom of the night.

Termites and white ants, which had been sleeping through the hot season, emerged from their lairs. Out of every hole, crevice and crack, huge winged ants emerged, at first fluttering about heavily, on this, the first and last flight of their lives. There was only one direction in which they could fly, towards the light—towards electric bulbs and street lamps and kerosene lanterns throughout the city. The street lamp beneath our room attracted a massive swarm of clumsy termites, which gave the impression of one thick, slowly revolving body.

It was the hour of lizards. They had their reward for weeks of patient waiting. Plying their sticky pink tongues, they devoured insects swiftly. For hours they crammed their stomachs, knowing that such a feast would not be theirs again till the next season. Throughout the entire hot season the insect world prepares for this flight out of darkness into light, but not one survives its bid for freedom.

Drowsy, I closed my eyes, but the sounds of the city's unceasing traffic came through the window. Ships and distant ports seemed very far away but so did hills and mountain streams.

I fell asleep and woke up only when Daljit returned.

'I've solved our problem!' he said, beaming. 'We won't bother with the train. I got friendly with a truck driver, and he has offered to take us as far as Jaipur. That's nearly 300 miles. It will be quite safe to take a train from Jaipur.'

'When can your friend take us?'

'The truck leaves at four o'clock in the morning.'

'There's no rest for the wicked,' I said. 'Still, the less time we lose the better. It's Wednesday, and my uncle's ship might sail on Saturday. What will we have to pay?'

'Nothing. It's a free ride. The driver is a Sikh, and I persuaded him that we are related to each other through the marriage of my brother-in-law to his sister-in-law's niece!'

At four the next morning we made our way towards the Red Fort, its ramparts dark against the starry sky. The streets which had been teeming with so much life the previous evening were now deserted. The street lamps shed lonely pools of light on the pavements. The occasional car glided silently past, but it belonged to another kind of world altogether.

Near the Fort we found a couple of dhabas which were still open. They did business with the truck drivers who slept by day and drove by night.

Our driver, a tall, bearded Sikh, loomed over us out of the darkness. He had a companion with him, also a Sikh, who was still in his underwear.

'You can get in at the back,' said the driver in his thick Punjabi, which I could follow sufficiently well. 'We'll be off in a few minutes.'

The truck was parked beneath a peepul tree. We pulled ourselves up into the back of the open truck, only to find our way barred by what seemed at first to be a prehistoric monster.

The monster snorted once, stamped heavily on the boards, and sent us tumbling backwards.

'*Bhaiyyaji*!' cried Daljit to the driver. 'There's some kind of animal in here!'

'Don't worry, it's only Mumta,' said our friend.

'But what is it doing in here?'

'She is going with us. I am taking her to the market in Jaipur. So get in with her boys, and make yourselves comfortable.'

There was now enough light to enable us to take a closer look at our travelling companion. She was a full-grown buffalo from the Punjab.

'An excellent buffalo,' said Daljit, who appeared to be familiar with the finer points of these animals. 'Notice her blue eyes!'

'I didn't know buffaloes had blue eyes,' I said dryly.

'Only the best buffaloes have them,' said Daljit. 'Blue-eyed buffaloes give more milk than brown-eyed ones.'

Fortunately for us, the Sardarji started the truck and an early morning breeze, blowing across the river, swept away some of the stench so typical of buffaloes.

We were soon out of Delhi and bowling along at a fair speed on the road to Jaipur. The recent rain had waterlogged low-lying areas, and the herons, cranes and snipe were numerous. Fields and trees were alive with strange, beautiful birds: the long-tailed king crow, blue jays and weaver birds, and occasionally the great white-headed kite, which is said to be Garuda, God Vishnu's famous steed.

As we travelled further into Rajasthan, the peacocks became more numerous, so did the camels loping along the side of the road in straight, orderly lines. And, as the vegetation grew less and the desert took over, the people themselves grew more colourful, as though to make up for the absence of colour in the landscape. The women wore wide red skirts, and gold and silver ornaments. They were handsome, tall, fair and strong. The men were tall too and the older among them had flowing white beards.

As the day grew older, and the sun rose higher in the sky, the traffic on the road increased, but our truck driver, instead of slowing down, drove faster.

Perhaps he was in a hurry to dispose of the buffalo. Soon he was trying to overtake another truck.

The truck in front was moving fast too, and its driver had no intention of giving up the middle of the road. It was piled high with stacks of sugarcane.

'It's going to be a race!' cried Daljit excitedly, standing up against the buffalo, in order to get a better view.

The road was not wide enough to take two large vehicles at once, and as the other truck wouldn't make way, ours had to fall in behind it, almost suffocating us with the exhaust fumes. We were thrown to the

floorboards as the truck lurched over the ruts in the rough road, and Mumta, getting nervous, almost trampled upon us. Then there was a tremendous bump, a grinding of brakes, and we came to a stop.

As the dust cleared, we made out our driver's bearded face gazing anxiously down at us.

'Are you all right?' he asked gruffly.

'I think so,' I said.

'Did you overtake the other truck?' asked Daljit.

'No,' grunted our friend. 'He would not give way. He was a Sikh, too. You had better come in front.'

We agreed without any hesitation and his assistant rather grudgingly joined the buffalo.

After a few miles, the driver became friendly and told us that his name was Gurnam Singh.

'Would you like to hear my new horn?' he asked in Punjabi.

'Have we not been hearing it all this time?' I asked rather pointedly in Hindi. We got along well enough.

'You can't hear it well in the back,' he said, quite oblivious to what I meant. 'That's why I've brought you here in front. What do you think of it?' he asked, as a shattering sound filled the cabin of the truck.

'It is a fine horn,' I said, fingers in my ears. 'It could not be louder.'

'You can hear it half a mile ahead,' said Gurnam

Singh proudly, and he blasted off at two young men who were sharing a bicycle. They moved out of the way with alacrity.

'It makes a lot of noise in here, too,' I said, and added hastily, for fear of offending him, 'not that it matters, of course . . .'

'Doesn't your horn have more than one tone of voice?' asked Daljit.

I thought this was a bit rude, but Gurnam Singh seemed to welcome the question.

'Two!' he exclaimed. 'Male and female. See.' And he produced a high note and then a low note, both equally ear-shattering. Ahead of us, a camel ran off the road and into the fields.

'This is a terrific horn,' said Gurnam Singh. 'I've had it made specially for this truck. No foreign horns for me. They are not loud enough. Indian horns are the best!'

In an interval of comparative quiet, I found myself reflecting on the nature of sound—the unpleasantness of some sounds, and the sweetness of others, and why certain sounds (like those made by monster-horns) can be sweet to some and terrible to others.

'It was made in Old Delhi,' continued Gurnam Singh, interrupting my thoughts with further comment on his horn. 'Seventy-five rupees only. Made by hand,

to my own specifications. There is only one drawback—
it mustn't get wet!'

As his fist came down on the horn again, I thought
of praying for rain, but the sky was quite clear and I
decided that such a prayer would be an unreasonable and
ungrateful demand considering the huge kindness this
man was showing us by letting us ride with him so far.

'Ah, but you don't know what it is to have a horn
like mine. Try it, friend. Why don't you try it for
yourself?'

The question was addressed to me, as I was sitting
beside him, Daljit being near the door.

'Oh, that is quite all right,' I said. 'You have already
proved its excellence.'

'No, you must try it. I insist that you try it!' He
was like a big boy, suddenly generous, determined to
share a new toy with a younger brother.

He grabbed my right hand and placed it on the
horn, and, as I felt it give a little, a thrill of pleasure
rushed up my arm. I pressed hard, and a stream of
music flowed in and out of the truck. And as I kept
pressing down, I experienced the driver's happiness,
for, with a horn like his, one felt the power and glory
that belongs to the kings of the road.

❖

It was getting dark by the time we reached Jaipur, so we were not able to see much of the city. We spent the night in the truck, sleeping in the back with Gurnam Singh. Mumta had been disposed of on the way. Jaipur nights can be chilly, even in summer, so Gurnam Singh considerately shared his bedding with us. Because he was accustomed to sleeping in the body of the truck, he was soon asleep, snoring loudly and rhythmically. Daljit and I tossed and turned restlessly. He kicked me several times in the night. The floor of the truck was hard, and retained various buffalo smells.

We had hardly fallen asleep (or so it seemed), when Gurnam Singh woke us up, saying that it was almost four o'clock and that he had to start on his return journey, this time with a load of red sandstone.

'What a life!' exclaimed Daljit, sleepily rubbing his eyes with one hand. 'I'd hate to be a truck driver.'

'One has to live somehow,' philosophized Gurnam Singh. 'I like driving. I knew how to drive when I was merely six or seven. The money is not so bad, either. Now, when I get back to Delhi, I will have two days off, which I will spend with my wife and children. Goodbye friends, and if you pass through Delhi again, you will find me near the walls of the Red Fort.'

We waved to him as he shot off in his truck, throwing up huge clouds of dust, making a great noise and probably waking the local inhabitants. Dogs barked, and a cock began to crow.

We were on the outskirts of the city, facing a large lake. On the other side was open country, bare hills and desert. We could also make out the ruins of a building—probably a palace or a hunting lodge—among some thorn bushes and babul trees.

'Let's go out there,' suggested Daljit. 'We can bathe in the lake and rest. Then later in the morning we can come into the city and find out about trains.'

We set out along the shores of the lake, and it was a good half hour before we reached the opposite bank.

There was no one in the fields, but a camel was going round and round a well, drawing up water in small trays. Smoke rose from houses in a nearby village, and the notes of a flute floated over to us on the still morning air.

It took us about twenty minutes to reach the ruin, which seemed like an old hunting lodge put up by some Rajput prince when game must have been plentiful.

The gate of the lodge was blocked with rubble, but part of the wall had crumbled apart and we climbed through the gap and found ourselves in a stone-paved courtyard in the centre of which stood a dry, disused stone fountain. A small peepul tree was growing from the cracks in the floor of the fountain.

We crossed the courtyard to the main structure,

and then Daljit stopped and asked: 'Do you smell something, Rusty?'

'Yes,' I said, 'curry.'

This was the last thing we expected to find. It meant the ruin was inhabited. I wondered if it would be better to turn around and leave, but curiosity got the better of us—curiosity, and the tantalizing aroma of curry! So Daljit and I moved forward, out of the sun and into the shade of a covered veranda. A door led into a dark chamber from which the curry smells appeared to be wafting across, and there we stood, hesitating on the brink of the unknown.

'Well, go ahead,' prompted Daljit.

'I was waiting for you,' I said, feeling a bit apprehensive for no clear reason.

Smiling at each other in mutual understanding, we stepped into the room together and found it empty.

There was a *choolah* in one corner, and on it stood a pot in which something delicious was cooking. Of the cook there was no sign.

I moved warily towards the fire, lifted the lid off the pot, and sniffed. Chicken curry! Chicken curry in a ruined hunting lodge in the middle of nowhere! We didn't stop to wonder how or why it had got there. There weren't any utensils about, so we dipped our fingers into the curry and I had just sunk my teeth into a fleshy bit when a pair of strong arms came around from behind and lifted me off my feet.

I was so startled that I dropped the piece of chicken. I struggled to get free from the other's grip but his arms were very powerful. That they were a man's arms and not a ghost's I could tell by the black hair on his forearm. I struggled and kicked about wildly, and then someone, another man, loomed up in front of me and grabbed me by the legs. I could hear Daljit struggling with someone else, and tried to shout to him, but the man who held me by my legs stuck an oily rag into my mouth. He caught my hands and held them while my feet were tied together with a length of rope. I was dumped on the ground, face downwards, with my hands and feet in ropes. Daljit, I saw, was in much the same position at the other end of the room. There wasn't much we could do. There were at least three men with us.

'He's only a boy,' said one of the men, in the local dialect of Hindi (which to my surprise I found I understood), bending over and examining my face. In the darkness of the room I could not make out his features, but I knew he had a beard, because I had felt it on my neck, and his breath smelt strongly of garlic.

'Boy, man or girl,' said another, 'whoever tries to make off with our food deserves a good thrashing.'

'He is quite fair, this one,' said the bearded man.

'Is he a foreigner?'

'Yes, he looks like one. Let us take them into the courtyard. We'll be able to see them better outside.'

'No, we mustn't show ourselves! If the villagers spot us in here, word would soon get around. We want to use this place again, don't we?'

'Light the lamp, then.'

The man who set to work lighting a kerosene lantern was the tallest man in the group. As the flame in the lantern shot up, it cast a huge shadow on the wall. This man was a giant, several inches over six feet. He was bare-chested, and his hair was close-cropped. His muscles stood out like lumps of iron. Another man behind the bearded one appeared to be the one giving the orders; I could not see him as yet.

'Turn him over so that we can have a good look,' he said.

The giant rolled me over on the ground, so that I was staring helplessly at the blackened ceiling. A few moments later three faces were staring down at me. At their mercy in that dark, dark room, tied, gagged and trussed up, I was quaking with fear. They looked like criminals. Probably they were dacoits, using the ruin as a hideout.

The bearded man had high cheekbones and slanting eyes. The giant did not have a cruel face, inspite of his broad nose and thick, heavy lips. It was the third man who frightened me most. He wasn't big and he wasn't ugly. He was, in fact, rather short, and he was smiling down at me, but it was a smile that sent a shiver down my spine.

'It wasn't very nice of you to help yourself to our chicken,' he said in a smooth voice. 'Not after Bhambiri here went to so much trouble to steal it.'

'Yes, in the middle of the night,' said the giant, who had the quaint name of Bhambiri, which means spinning top. 'I had three dogs and half the village chasing me through the fields. But I gave them the slip!' And he chuckled hugely to himself.

'It's all very well to make a joke of it,' said the bearded one with a look of gloom. 'The chicken isn't important. Why did they really come here? What do you think they know?'

'Let's ask this one,' said the short, sinister man. He bent down, stared hard into my eyes and then pulled the rag out of my mouth. No sooner had the gag gone than I felt something cold and hard against my lower teeth. It was like a dentist making a preliminary examination of his patient's teeth, but this short, sinister man was doing it with point of a dagger.

'Don't talk or shout except when we tell you,' he warned. Then, taking the knife away he stood back. 'Let him sit up a little. Do you understand me?'

I nodded. Bhambiri came forward, and lifting me with ease, set me up against the wall.

'My wrists are hurting,' I said.

Bhambiri made as if to untie my hands, but his leader said: 'Don't untie him, you fool,' and the giant moved away.

'Now. Tell us what you are doing here.'

'We were just looking for a place to rest,' I said, deciding that there was no harm in telling the truth.

'Twist his arm, Bhambiri.'

I don't think the giant meant to twist my arm very hard, but even the slight wrench he gave it made me cry out. He had obviously been a wrestler at some point in his career.

'Don't lie!' spat out the leader. 'It's very painful to lie. You've been spying on us.'

'We do not know anything about you,' I said desperately. 'We have only been in Jaipur one night.'

'They're only boys.'

'We are on our way to the coast,' I said. 'We do not have much money.'

'So you were about to steal our food,' said Bhambiri sternly. A lost meal concerned him more than the possibility of our being police spies.

'Let's see if they have any money on them,' said the short one. He went through my pockets and produced the few notes and loose change that I possessed. Then he went over to Daljit, still gagged and helpless, took his wallet, examined it and said: 'There's thirty or forty here.' He put everything into his own pockets. I was dismayed. Now what were we to do?

'Shall I let them go now?' asked Bhambiri.

'No, you idiot, they'll set up an alarm. We should just finish what's left of the food, and then be off.'

So we lay there, trussed up for about fifteen minutes, while the dacoits finished their meal. I could see that Daljit, like me, was itching to be set free and leave this horrible place for ever. Meanwhile, it looked as if the dacoits had no intention of leaving anything behind, and when they finished, they licked their fingers and belched. I couldn't help thinking that Bhambiri had a wonderful belch. It came from deep down in his belly, gathered volume as it rose to the surface, and then resounded round the chamber as though a gong had been struck. The short one belched very quietly, in his mean way.

'We'll leave them here,' he said, giving me a narrow sly smile. 'They can have as much rest as they like. They won't be found for a day or two, perhaps. Close the fair boy's mouth again, Bhambiri.'

The giant bent over me, shutting off the light from the lantern and though it was dark I thought I had detected a glimmer of sympathy in his eyes. He thrust the dirty rag back into my mouth and made it fast with a strip of cloth. And then, while he still had me away from the light, he slipped his hands behind my back and swiftly loosened the knot of the rope that bound my hands.

'All right, let's go,' said the leader.

He walked out of the chamber, followed by the others. Bhambiri went out last but he did not look back at us. I waited until I could no longer hear their footsteps and then I slipped my hands out of the rope that Bhambiri had loosened, and wrenched the gag off my mouth. I managed to free my feet, and then crawled over to Daljit. I removed his gag, then started on the rope round his wrists.

'How did you get loose?' he asked, as soon as he was able to find his voice.

'Don't talk too loudly,' I said. 'They might return. Their cooking pots are still here, though they probably belong to someone else.'

'But how did you get loose, Rusty?'

'The big fellow freed my hands when the others weren't looking. I think he felt sorry for us.'

'God bless his soft heart,' said Daljit fervently. 'We might have been lying here for days starving to death. Or dying of thirst, whichever happens first.'

He sat up as soon as his limbs were free, and began stretching his arms and legs. Then he brought his knees up to his chin and gave me an anxious look.

'What do we do now, Rusty? They've taken our money. We can't go anywhere, forward or backward. We'll have to give ourselves up at the nearest police station.'

'They have taken our haversacks, too. Well, if they're dacoits, I suppose it's their business to take what they can. I suppose we should consider ourselves lucky. They might have murdered us.'

'We wouldn't have been their first victims. That short fellow . . .' Daljit, with a scowl on his face, was considering the possibilities; then, his hands in his pockets, his face brightened. 'They weren't so clever, Rusty. They forgot my watch, just imagine, and there's still some change in one of my pockets!'

'Well, that's something,' I said. 'We won't starve. We can always sell the watch. But if we can get to Jamnagar somehow without selling it . . . We should keep it in case of a real emergency.'

'Isn't this an emergency?'

'I suppose so. Still . . .'

'And you think we can go on? You haven't given up yet?'

'What about you?'

'Do you think I'm likely to give up before you? Come on, Rusty, let's get out of here. It's Saturday tomorrow and we have to get to that ship!'

Daljit and I lay stretched out on the floor of a goods wagon, which was open to the sky. The train jogged slowly through the desert, and hot winds blew the sand in upon us. The gritty sand got in our hair and into our eyes and mouths. There was no escape from it. Daljit's face, caked with sand, was the same colour as mine. The sun beat down on us mercilessly and there was only a small corner of the wagon which gave us some shade. We had bought some bananas with what was left of our money, and we took bites on them from time to time.

'We'll be half starved by morning,' I said. 'I think we should save something of these bananas.'

'Morning comes tomorrow,' said Daljit. 'I'm hungry today. Besides, we'll reach Jamnagar in the morning.'

'And if the ship has gone?' I couldn't help wondering about all the possible situations we might find ourselves in—even if they weren't what we hoped for.

'The ship will be there.' Daljit was, as usual, confident about everything.

'How do you know?' I asked.

'I don't. I'm just an optimist.'

'It will sail any day now. Perhaps it has left already. Daljit, we'll be stuck without any money; what will we do then?'

'Stop worrying, Rusty. Don't be so nervous. If we're in trouble, we'll sell the watch and go back to school and be expelled. No, they won't expel us—they'll lose all my father's money—but if you like, we can run away again.'

'That ship had better be there,' I muttered.

'It will be there. We'll be off in it tomorrow. I hope you will come and live with me in Mombasa for some time.'

'Oh, I'll probably be too busy travelling with my uncle,' I said.

'How wonderful! No more school. I may come with you, Rusty. I don't think business will be very interesting.'

'We could see the world together,' I said. 'What dreamers we are!'

'Well, we are on our way somewhere. As my grandfather used to say (he was the grandfather who travelled round the world selling cloth made in the Punjab), "The best reason for going from one place to another is to see what's in between."'

'He sold cloth in between,' I said. 'He wasn't dreaming like us.'

'You're giving up, Rusty.'

'No, I'm not.'

But it was a hard night's journey. The train was agonizingly slow and stopped at many places. At one small station, a number of sacks filled with what must have been cattle-fodder were tossed into the wagon, almost burying us in our fitful sleep. But we found they were comfortable to rest on and lay stretched out on top of them until the first light of morning.

As the sky cleared, we knew we were not far from our journey's end. The landscape had undergone a complete change. We had left the desert for the coastal plain.

The tall waving palms parted, and then I spotted the sea.

It was the sea as I had always dreamt of it ever since my days in Kathiawar with my father. It was vast, lonely and blue, blue as the sky was blue, and the first ship I saw was a sailing ship, an Arab dhow, listing slightly in the mild breeze that blew onto the shore.

The train stopped at a small bridge spanning a stream which wound its way across the plain down to the sea.

We got down here, and waved our thanks to the brakesman who had tolerated our presence on the train. Then we slid down the banks of the stream, and hid beneath the bridge until the train moved off again. We didn't want the guard to see us; he might not be as tolerant as the brakesman.

Seeing that no one was about, we removed our dusty,

travel-stained clothes, and waded out into the stream, pushing our way through a tangle of water lilies. The current was sluggish unlike the swift streams in the hills, and the warm water was not as invigorating as the water we were used to from the mountain springs, but it was fresh enough for our purpose, and brought new life into our weary bodies. We thrashed about, splashing away and ducking each other, and Daljit, trying to swim underwater, came up with a water lily clinging to his long hair, which had come undone.

We stayed in the water for about fifteen minutes, and by then had lost all awareness of our surroundings. When we finally climbed back on the bank, we got a rude shock: our clothes were missing. Daljit's turban was all that remained.

Higher up the bank, three boys, clad only in loincloths, stood staring down at us. The biggest of them held out our clothes teasingly.

'Please bring us our clothes,' said Daljit good-naturedly in Hindi. 'It is kind of you to leave my turban, but I do not wear a turban anywhere except on my head!'

The three boys burst into laughter and turned on their heels, ambling away through the fields.

'Come back!' shouted Daljit.

'Let's go after them,' I said.

It was almost a matter of life and death for us. All that Daljit had on his person was his turban and his watch, but I didn't even have that much. We scrambled up the bank and ran in desperate pursuit of the boys. But they had had a good start, and knew their way through the fields. They had reached the village while we were still struggling through the field, tripping over culverts and irrigation ditches. A shower of pebbles, thrown at us from behind a wall, brought us to a stop.

'Let's try persuasion,' I suggested. Cupping my hands to my mouth, I shouted: 'Please give us back our clothes, we do not have any others!' I took the trouble to use my best Hindi.

The only response was a large stone, which flew past my ear.

'I don't think they speak Hindi here,' I told Daljit. 'Shall I try English? I don't know any other language.' 'Not English! It will only result in more stones. I suppose they speak Gujarati . . . and I don't know any.'

A man appeared at the edge of the field, waving a stick at us and shouting incomprehensibly.

'What do you think he's saying?' asked Daljit.

'How should I know? He probably wants us to get off his land.'

'Well, we're not going without our clothes.'

'I think we are,' I said. 'Here come the dogs!'

Several village dogs, baying like the hounds of the Baskervilles, came bounding towards us, followed by two men with sticks and several boys with stones. Daljit and I lost no time in presenting them with a rear view, and we made off through the fields as fast as our weary limbs would take us. It wasn't until we had crossed the stream again that we paused for breath. The villagers did not follow us across, so we concluded that we were now on someone else's land. The village men shook their sticks at us and we shook our fists at them, but we were still without our clothes. We left the stream and took shelter in a grove of mango trees. There, we were left alone.

'And now what do we do?' Daljit wanted to know.

'Wearing nothing, you mean?'

'Why not? We'll wait until it gets dark.'

'And when morning comes?'

'Oh, we'll find something. We can sell my watch and buy some clothes.'

'I can't imagine walking into a shop wearing nothing but a watch, which we then offer for sale.'

'We can pretend to be sadhus,' he said. 'Or at least the disciples of sadhus, *chelas*. It's the fashion these days. Only the best sadhus go about naked. We might even be given free board and lodging for the night.'

'And by the morning we'd find the ship has sailed without us.'

'I hadn't thought of that . . .'

But as we sat there discussing our predicament we saw two men, probably railway workers, walking down to the stream on our side of it. They wore trousers and shirts and shoes unlike the farmers who wore dhotis. At first I thought they were going to the stream to drink water, but when I saw them removing their clothes, I sat up with a wild hope.

'Daljit,' I said urgently, 'do you see them?'

'Of course I see them.' He was not slow in grasping what I meant. 'Yes, this is our only chance, Rusty. We must show no mercy, remember! This world is no place for gentlemen like us. We must change our ways, and do as the local people do! They will probably blame the villagers. But move quietly.'

'Let's keep to the bushes. They mustn't see us!'

Crawling along on all fours, heedless of the thorns that scratched our bare flesh, we approached the stream again, at the approximate place where the men were bathing. They were making a fair noise as they romped about in the water like boys (bathing in the open seems to make adults quite skittish, I've noticed, perhaps because they are back in the element from which mankind first emerged as playful amoebae!) and did not see or hear us. Their clothes lay in an untidy heap a few yards away.

'I'll get them,' whispered Daljit. 'If they see me, they'll mistake me for a boy from the village. But if they see you, we've had it!'

He dashed out from the bushes with great speed (and if he had shown the same spirit in school, he would have made a good athlete), swept up all the clothes in his arms, and scrambled back to me. 'Brilliant!' I whispered. 'They didn't see a thing.' We didn't wait for them to discover their loss (though we were sorely tempted to do so), but took to our heels and fled back through the mango grove.

We crossed the railway tracks and ran across the open countryside until we got to an old well, and there, in the generous shade of an ancient banyan tree, we got into our new clothes, which were several sizes too big for us. But who cared about that anyway? At least we were not naked anymore!

Two hours later we were at Jamnagar.

We stopped near a small tea shop and watched other people eating laddoos and bhelpuri. We couldn't even afford a coconut.

'Where is the harbour?' I asked the shopkeeper.

'Two miles from here,' he replied.

'Are there any ships in the port?' I asked, relieved yet anxious.

'What do you want with a ship?'

'What does anyone want with a ship?'

'Well there's only one and it sails today, so you had better hurry if you want to go away on it'

'Let's go,' said Daljit

'Wait!' said a young man who was lounging against the counter. 'It will take you almost an hour to get there if you walk. I will take you in my cart.' He pointed to a shabby pony-cart close by. The pony did not look as though it wanted to go anywhere.

'My pony is fast!' said the young man, following our glances. 'Never go by appearances. She may look tired but she runs like a champion! Get in, friends, I will charge you only one rupee.'

'We don't have any money,' I said. 'We'll walk.'

'Fifty paisa, then,' he said. 'Fifty paisa and a glass of tea. Jump in my friends!'

'All right,' agreed Daljit. 'There's no time to lose. Fifty paisa and buy your own tea.'

We climbed into the cart, and the youth jumped up in front and cracked his whip. The pony lurched forward, the wheels rattled and shook, and we set off down the bazaar road at a tremendous trot.

'I didn't know you had fifty paisa left,' I said.

'I don't,' Daljit replied. 'But we'll worry about that later. Your uncle can pay!'

As soon as we were out of the town and on the open road to the sea, the pony went faster. She couldn't help doing so, as the road was downhill. The wind blew my hair across my eyes, and the salty tang of the sea was in the air.

Daljit shook me in his excitement.

'We will soon be at the harbour,' he yelled joyfully. 'And then away at last!'

The driver called out endearments to his pony, and, exhilarated by the sea breeze and the comparative speed of his carriage, he burst into song. As we turned a bend in the road, the seafront came into view. There were several small dhows close to the shore, and fishing boats were beached on the sand. The fishermen were drying their nets while their children ran naked in the surf. A steamer stood out on the sea and though I could not make out its name from that distance, I was sure it was the *Iris*.

The cart stopped at the beginning of the pier, and we tumbled out and began running along the pier. But even as we ran, it became clear to me that the ship was moving away from us, moving out to the sea. Its propeller sent small waves rippling back to the pier.

'Captain!' I shouted. 'Uncle Jim! Wait for us!'

A lascar standing in the stern waved to us, but that was all. I stood at the end of the pier, waving my hands and shouting into the wind.

'Captain! Uncle Jim! Wait for us!'

Nobody answered. The seagulls, wheeling in the wake of the steamer, seemed to take up the cry— 'Captain, Captain . . .'

The ship drew further away, gaining speed. And still I called to it in a hoarse, pleading voice.

Yokohama, San Diego, Valparaiso, London, all slipping away for ever . . .

We stood by ourselves on the pier, in the late afternoon, with gulls wheeling around us, mocking us with their calls. A phrase from one of Uncle Jim's letters ran through my head. 'First call Aden, then Suez and up the Canal . . .' But for me there was only the long journey back, the indignation of my guardian, the boredom of the classroom and the misery of boarding school.

Daljit had been silent. When at last I forced myself to look at him, I was surprised to see him smiling. He did not seem at all downcast.

'We've arrived too late,' I said. 'We've come hundreds of miles, and we're five minutes too late!'

'Never mind!'

'Everything has been for nothing, Daljit. All our plans . . . all our dreams!'

'What's wrong with dreams? Nothing. As long as they don't come true, we can keep on dreaming. We'll go back to school and we'll have other dreams.'

'I didn't know you were a philosopher, Daljit. And how do you think we are going to get back to school? Even if you sell your watch, it won't be enough. I'm fed up. I don't want to go anywhere. I'll sit on this pier until my uncle returns.'

'How long will you have to wait?'

'One or two years,' I said, smiling.

'Don't worry about getting back,' said Daljit reassuringly. 'When we ran away, it had to be secret, but it isn't a secret any more. We'll sell the watch, pay the cart driver, and send a telegram!'

'To the principal?'

'No. To an uncle of mine in Bombay. He can come and fetch us in his car. And he can take us back to school too by car. We'll travel in comfort this time! We'll eat chicken and have ice cream all the way. We'll enjoy ourselves for a few days!'

'Yes,' I said gloomily. 'We won't have anything to enjoy when we get back.'

I didn't say much else as we walked back to the cart. My thoughts were far away. I told myself that next year, some time, Uncle Jim would return in the *Iris*, and then I wouldn't make another mistake. I'd be on the ship long before it sailed.

And so I stopped and stared out at the sea for the last time. The steamer looked very small in that vast expanse of ocean.

This year, next year, some time . . . Yokohama, Valparaiso, San Diego, London . . .

The Playing Fields of Simla

IT HAD BEEN a lonely winter for a sixteen-year-old. I had spent the first few weeks of the vacation with my guardian and his wife in Dehra. Then they left for Delhi, and I was pretty much on my own. Of course, the servants were there to take care of my needs, but there was no one to keep me company. I would wander off in the mornings taking some path up the hills, come back home for lunch, read a bit and then stroll off again till it was time for dinner. Sometimes I walked up to my grandparents' house, but it seemed so different now—with people I didn't know occupying the house. At those times I felt as if I had never ever lived in that house or loved it the way I actually had. The three-month winter break over, I was almost eager to return to my boarding school in Simla. No, I wasn't at Arundel anymore—not after that 'running-away-from-school-fiasco'. When we (Daljit and I) got back to

Arundel, his father and my guardian were summoned. We were reprimanded, and rusticated without much delay. Now I stayed and studied at a better school—it *was* a better school, for I was surely happier there.

It wasn't as though I had many friends at school. I needed a friend but it was not easy to find one among a horde of rowdy, pea-shooting eighth formers, who carved their names on desks and stuck chewing gum on the class teacher's chair. Had I grown up with other children, I might have developed a taste for schoolboy anarchy, but, in sharing my father's loneliness after his separation from my mother, and in being bereft of any close family ties, I had turned into a premature adult. The mixed nature of my reading—Dickens, Richmal Crompton, Tagore and *Champion* and *Film Fun* comics—probably reflected the confused state of my life. A book reader was rare even in those pre-electronic times. On rainy days most boys played cards or Monopoly, or listened to Artie Shaw on the wind-up gramophone in the common room.

After a month in the eighth form I began to notice a new boy, Omar, and then only because he was a quiet, almost taciturn person who took no part in the form's feverish attempts to imitate the Marx Brothers at the circus. He showed no resentment at the prevailing anarchy, nor did he make a move to participate in it. Once he caught me looking at him, and he smiled ruefully, tolerantly. Did I sense another adult in the class? Someone who was a little older than his years?

Even before we began talking to each other, Omar and I developed an understanding of sorts, and we'd nod almost respectfully to each other when we met in the classroom corridors or the environs of the dining hall or the dormitory. We were not in the same house. The house system practised its own form of apartheid, whereby a member of, say, Curzon House was not expected to fraternize with someone belonging to Rivaz or Lefroy! Those public schools certainly knew how to clamp you into compartments. However, these barriers vanished when Omar and I found ourselves selected for the School Colts' hockey team—Omar as a full-back, I as goalkeeper.

The taciturn Omar now spoke to me occasionally, and we combined well on the field of play. A good understanding is needed between goalkeeper and full-back. We were on the same wavelength. I anticipated his moves, he was familiar with mine. Years later, when I read Conrad's *The Secret Sharer*, I thought of Omar.

It wasn't until we were away from the confines of school, classroom and dining hall that our friendship flourished. The hockey team travelled to Sanawar on the next mountain range, where we were to play a couple of matches against our old rivals, the Lawrence Royal Military School. This had been my father's old school, so I was keen to explore its grounds and peep into its classrooms.

Omar and I were thrown together a good deal during the visit to Sanawar, and in our more leisurely moments, strolling undisturbed around a school where we were guests and not pupils, we exchanged life histories and other confidences. Omar, too, had lost his father—had I sensed that before?—shot in some tribal encounter on the Frontier, for he hailed from the lawless lands beyond Peshawar. A wealthy uncle was seeing to Omar's education.

We wandered into the school chapel, and there I found my father's name—A.A. Bond—on the school's roll of honour board: old boys who had lost their lives while serving during the two World Wars.

'What did his initials stand for?' asked Omar.

'Aubrey Alexander.'

'Unusual names, like yours. Why did your parents call you Rusty?'

'I am not sure.' I told him about the book I was writing. It was my first one and was called *Nine Months* (the length of the school term, not a pregnancy), and it described some of the happenings at school and lampooned a few of our teachers. I had filled three slim exercise books with this premature literary project, and I allowed Omar to go through them. He must have been my first reader and critic. 'They're very interesting,' he said, 'but you'll get into trouble if someone finds them. Specially Mr Oliver.' And he read out an offending verse—*Oily, Oily, Oily, with his balls on a trolley, And his arse all painted green!*

I have to admit it wasn't great literature. I was better at hockey and football. I made some spectacular saves, and we won our matches against Sanawar. When we returned to Simla, we were school heroes for a couple of days and lost some of our reticence; we were even a little more forthcoming with other boys. And then Mr Fisher, my housemaster, discovered my literary opus, *Nine Months,* under my mattress, and took it away and read it (as he told me later) from cover to cover. Corporal punishment then being in vogue, I was given six of the best with a springy malacca cane, and my manuscript was torn up and deposited in Mr Fisher's waste-paper basket. All I had to show for my efforts were some purple welts on my bottom. These were proudly displayed to all who were interested, and I was a hero for another two days.

'Will you go away too when the British leave India?' Omar asked me one day.

'I don't think so,' I said. 'I don't have anyone to go back to in England, and my guardian, Mr Harrison, too seems to have no intention of going back.'

'Everyone is saying that our leaders and the British are going to divide the country. Simla will be in India, Peshawar in Pakistan!'

'Oh, it won't happen,' I said glibly. 'How can they cut up such a big country?' But even as we chatted about the possibility, Nehru and Jinnah and Mountbatten and all those who mattered were preparing their instruments for major surgery.

Before their decision impinged on our lives and everyone else's, we found a little freedom of our own—in an underground tunnel that we discovered below the third flat.

It was really part of an old, disused drainage system, and when Omar and I began exploring it, we had no idea just how far it extended. After crawling along on our bellies for some twenty feet, we found ourselves in complete darkness. Omar had brought along a small pencil torch, and with its help we continued writhing forward (moving backwards would have been quite impossible) until we saw a glimmer of light at the end of the tunnel. Dusty, musty, very scruffy, we emerged at last on to a grassy knoll, a little way outside the school boundary.

It's always a great thrill to escape beyond the boundaries that adults have devised. Here we were in unknown territory. To travel without passports—that would be the ultimate in freedom!

But more passports were on their way—and more boundaries.

Lord Mountbatten, viceroy and governor-general-to-be, came for our Founder's Day and gave away the prizes. I had won a prize for something or the other, and mounted the rostrum to receive my book from this towering, handsome man in his pinstripe suit. Bishop Cotton's was then the premier school of India, often referred to as the 'Eton of the East'. Viceroys and governors had graced its functions. Many of its boys had gone on to eminence in the civil services and armed forces. There was one 'old boy' about whom they maintained a stolid silence—General Dyer, who had ordered the massacre at Amritsar and destroyed the trust that had been building up between Britain and India.

Now Mountbatten spoke of the momentous events that were happening all around us—the War had just come to an end, the United Nations held out the promise of a world living in peace and harmony, and India, an equal partner with Britain, would be among the great nations . . .

A few weeks later, Bengal and the Punjab provinces were bisected. Riots flared up across northern India, and there was a great exodus of people crossing the newly-drawn frontiers of Pakistan and India. Homes were destroyed, thousands lost their lives.

The common-room radio and the occasional newspaper kept us abreast of events, but in our tunnel, Omar and I felt immune from all that was happening, worlds away from all the pillage, murder and revenge. And outside the tunnel, on the pine knoll below the school, there was fresh untrodden grass, sprinkled with clover and daisies, the only sounds we heard were the hammering of a woodpecker and the distant insistent call of the Himalayan barbet. Who could touch us there?

'And when all the wars are done,' I said, 'a butterfly will still be beautiful.'

'Did you read that somewhere?'

'No, it just came into my head.'

'Already you're a writer.'

'No, I want to play hockey for India or football for Arsenal. Only winning teams!'

'You can't win forever. Better to be a writer.' When the monsoon arrived, the tunnel was flooded, the drain choked with rubble. We were allowed out to the cinema to see Laurence Olivier's *Hamlet,* a film that did nothing to raise our spirits on a wet and gloomy afternoon, but it was our last picture that year, because communal riots suddenly broke out in Simla's Lower Bazaar, an area that was still much as Kipling had described it—'a man who knows his way there can defy all the police of India's summer capital'—and we were confined to school indefinitely.

112

One morning after prayers in the chapel, the headmaster announced that the Muslim boys—those who had their homes in what was now Pakistan—would have to be evacuated, sent to their homes across the border with an armed convoy.

The tunnel no longer provided an escape for us. The bazaar was out of bounds. The flooded playing field was deserted. Omar and I sat on a damp wooden bench and talked about the future in vaguely hopeful terms, but we didn't solve any problems. Mountbatten and Nehru and Jinnah were doing all the solving.

It was soon time for Omar to leave—he left along with some fifty other boys from Lahore, Pindi and Peshawar. The rest of us—Hindus, Christians, Parsis—helped them load their luggage into the waiting trucks. A couple of boys broke down and wept. So did our departing school captain, a Pathan who had been known for his stoic and unemotional demeanour. Omar waved cheerfully to me and I waved back. We had vowed to meet again some day.

The convoy got through safely enough. There was only one casualty—the school cook, who had strayed into an off-limits area in the foothill-town of Kalka and been set upon by a mob. He wasn't seen again.

Towards the end of the school year, just as we were all getting ready to leave for the school holidays,

I received a letter from Omar. He told me something about his new school and how he missed my company and our games and our tunnel to freedom. I replied and gave him my home address, but I did not hear from him again.

Some seventeen or eighteen years later I did get news of Omar, but in an entirely different context. India and Pakistan were at war and in a bombing raid over Ambala, not far from Simla, a Pakistani plane was shot down. Its crew died in the crash. One of them, I learnt later, was Omar.

Did he, I wonder, get a glimpse of the playing fields we knew so well as boys?

Perhaps memories of his school days flooded back as he flew over the foothills. Perhaps he remembered the tunnel through which we were able to make our little escape to freedom.

But there are no tunnels in the sky.

It Happened One Spring

THE LIGHT SPRING rain rode on the wind, into the trees, down the road; it brought an exhilarating freshness to the air, a smell of earth, a scent of flowers; it made me feel carefree and happy, and I smiled to myself as I walked along.

The long road wound round the hills, rose and fell and twisted down to Dehra; the road came from the mountains and passed through the jungle and valley and, after passing through Dehra, ended somewhere in the bazaar. But just where it ended no one knew, for the bazaar was a baffling place, where roads were easily lost.

I was three miles out of Dehra. The further I could get from Dehra, the happier I was likely to be. Just now I was only three miles out of Dehra, so I wasn't very happy, and, what was worse, I was walking homewards.

I felt good as the rain flecked my face; I liked

the smell and the freshness of it. I did not look at my surroundings or notice them—my mind, as usual, was very far away—but I felt their atmosphere, and I smiled again.

My mind was so very far away that it was a few minutes before I noticed the swish of bicycle wheels beside me. The cyclist did not pass me, but rode beside me, studying me, taking in every visible detail that I presented: the pale-faced adolescent with blue-grey eyes and fair hair; my face rough and marked, the lower lip hung loose and heavy. The way I walked (this was my usual style)—my hands in my pockets and my head bowed down. This gait of mine always gave me a deceptively tired appearance. I was a lazy person but not a tired one. The cyclist observed my bare head, the open-necked shirt, the flannel trousers, the sandals and the thick hide belt round my waist. A European was no longer a common sight in Dehra, but the cyclist was perhaps interested in meeting one.

'Hullo,' he said, giving his bell a tinkle.

I looked up properly now and saw a young, friendly face wrapped untidily in a turban.

'Hullo,' said the stranger, 'would you like me to ride you into town? If you are going to town?'

'No, I'm all right,' I replied, without slackening my pace. 'I like to walk.'

'So do I, but it's raining.'

And to support his argument, the rain fell harder.

'I like to walk in the rain,' I asserted. 'And I don't live in the town, I live outside it.'

Nice people didn't live *in* the town . . .

'Well, I can pass your way,' he persisted, determined to help me for some reason.

I looked again at this cyclist, who was dressed like me except for short pants and turban. His legs were long and athletic, his colour was an unusually rich gold, his features were fine, his mouth broke easily into friendliness. It was impossible to resist the warmth of his nature.

I pulled myself up on the crossbar, in front of him, and we moved off.

We rode slowly, gliding round the low hills, and soon the jungle on either side of the road began to give way to open fields and tea gardens and then to orchards and one or two houses.

'My name is Somi,' the cyclist said. 'Tell me when you reach your place. You stay with your parents?'

I considered the question too familiar for a stranger to ask, and made no reply.

'Do you like Dehra?' asked Somi. Obviously nothing was going to deter him from making conversation with me and satisfying his curiosity.

'Not much,' I said with pleasure.

'Well, after England it must seem dull . . .'

There was a pause and then I said: 'I haven't been to England. I was born here. I've never been anywhere else except Delhi, Kathiawar, Simla and Java.'

'Do you like Delhi?'

'Not much.'

We rode on in silence. The rain still fell, but the cycle moved smoothly over the wet road, making a soft, swishing sound.

Presently a man came in sight—no, it was not a man, it was a youth, but he had the appearance, the build of a man. He was walking towards town.

'Hey, Ranbir,' shouted Somi, as they neared the burly figure, 'want a lift?'

Ranbir ran into the road and slipped on to the carrier, behind Somi. The cycle wobbled a bit, but soon controlled itself and moved on, a little faster now.

Somi spoke into my ear: 'Meet my friend Ranbir. He is the best wrestler in the bazaar.'

'Hullo, mister,' said Ranbir, before I could even open my mouth.

'Hullo, mister,' I said, rather overwhelmed by his size and voice. Then Ranbir and Somi began a swift conversation in Hindi, and I felt a bit lost, even, for some strange reason, jealous of the newcomer.

Now someone was standing in the middle of the road, frantically waving his arms and shouting incomprehensibly.

'It is Suri,' said Somi.

It *was* Suri. He lived with his parents somewhere around our neighbourhood so I knew of him, though I hadn't ever met him personally.

Bespectacled and owlish to behold, Suri possessed an almost criminal cunning, and was both respected and despised by all who knew him. His interests were confined to people and their privacies (privacies which, when known to Suri, were soon made public).

He was a pale, bony, sickly boy, but he would probably live longer than Ranbir.

'Hey, give me a lift!' he shouted.

'Too many already,' said Somi.

'Oh, come on Somi, I'm nearly drowned.'

'It's stopped raining.'

'Oh, come on . . .'

So Suri climbed on to the handlebar, which rather obscured Somi's view of the road and caused the cycle to wobble all over the place. Ranbir kept slipping on and off the carrier, and I soon found the crossbar exceedingly uncomfortable. The cycle had barely been controlled when Suri started to complain.

'It hurts,' he whimpered.

119

'I haven't got a cushion,' said Somi.

'It is a cycle,' said Ranbir bitingly, 'not a Rolls Royce.'

Suddenly the road fell steeply, and the cycle gathered speed.

'Take it easy now,' said Suri, 'or I'll fly off!'

'Hold tight,' warned Somi. 'It's downhill nearly all the way. We will have to go fast because the brakes aren't very good.'

'Oh, Mummy!' wailed Suri.

'Shut up!' said Ranbir.

The wind hit us with a sudden force, and our clothes blew up like balloons, almost tearing us from the machine. I forgot my discomfort and clung desperately to the crossbar, too nervous to say a word. Suri howled and Ranbir kept telling him to shut up, but Somi was enjoying the ride. He laughed merrily, a clear, ringing laugh, a laugh that bore no malice and no derision but only enjoyment, fun . . .

'It's all right for you to laugh,' complained Suri. 'If anything happens, *I'll* get hurt!'

'If anything happens,' said Somi, 'we'll all get hurt!'

'That's right,' shouted Ranbir from behind.

I closed my eyes and muttered a quick prayer to God and put my trust in this cyclist who didn't seem to care about our fate . . .

'Oh, Mummy!' wailed Suri.

'Shut up!' said Ranbir.

The road twisted and turned as much as it could, and rose a little only to fall more steeply the other side. But eventually it began to even out, for we were nearing the town and almost in the residential area.

'The run is over,' said Somi, a little regretfully.

'Oh, Mummy!'

'Shut up.'

'I must get off now,' I said. 'I live very near.' Somi skidded the cycle to a standstill, and Suri shot off the handlebar into a muddy sidetrack. I slipped off, but Somi and Ranbir remained on their seats, Ranbir steadying the cycle with his feet on the ground.

'Well, thank you,' I said.

Somi said: 'Why don't you come and have your meal with us, there is not much further to go.'

I felt too shy and awkward to accept such an offer. After all, we weren't even friends. 'I've got to go home,' I murmured. 'I'm expected. Thanks very much.'

'Well, come and see us some time,' said Somi. 'If you come to the *chaat* shop in the bazaar, you are sure to find one of us. You know the bazaar?'

'Well, I have passed through it.'

I then began walking away, my hands once more in my pockets.

'Hey!' shouted Somi. 'You didn't tell us your name!'

I turned around hesitantly and then said, 'Rusty . . .'

'See you soon, Rusty,' yelled Somi, and the cycle pushed off.

I watched the cycle receding down the road, and Suri's shrill voice came to me on the wind. It had stopped raining, but I was actually aware of only one thing—that I was almost home, and that was a miserable thought. To my surprise and disgust, I found myself wishing that I had gone into Dehra with Somi.

I stood in the sidetrack and stared down the empty road, feeling immeasurably lonely.

I was standing in a corner of the missionary's garden admiring the riot of flowers that swayed in the gentle breeze. From that corner I could hear snatches of the conversation between the missionary's wife and my guardian.

'I hope you'll put the boy to work while I'm away,' he was saying. 'Make some use of him. He dreams too much. Most unfortunate that he's finished with school, I don't know what to do with him.'

'He doesn't know what to do with himself,' replied the missionary's wife. 'But I'll keep him occupied. He can do some weeding, or read to me in the afternoon. I'll keep an eye on him.'

'Good,' said Mr Harrison, my guardian. And, having cleared his conscience, he made quick his escape. He had totally forgotten about the fact that he had asked me to accompany him to the missionary's house, and that I was actually waiting for him in the garden!

Later, over lunch he told me:

'I'm going to Delhi tomorrow. Business.'

It was the only thing he said during the meal. When he had finished eating, he lit a cigarette and erected a curtain of smoke between himself and me. He was a heavy smoker, his fingers were stained a deep yellow.

'How long will you be gone, sir?' I asked, trying to sound casual.

Mr Harrison did not reply. He seldom answered my questions, and his own were stated, not asked; he probed and suggested, sharply, quickly, without ever encouraging loose conversation. He never talked about himself, he never argued, he would tolerate no argument. His wife had been in England for the last one year, so I was the sole recipient of all his monologues—whether they were conducted in instructions and commands, or fury and reprimands.

He was a tall man, neat in appearance, and, though over forty, looked younger because he kept his hair short, shaving above the ears. He had a small ginger toothbrush moustache.

I was afraid of my guardian.

Mr Harrison had done a lot for me. I can never deny this, yet this very fact made me afraid of him. I had been kept, fed and paid for, and sent to schools in the hills that were run on 'exclusively European lines'. I had, in a way, been bought by Mr Harrison. And now I felt that I was being owned by him. And that I must do only as my guardian wished.

I was ready to do as he wished: I had always obeyed him (except for that instance when I ran away from boarding school two years back). But I was ready to obey him not because I felt any respect for him, but because I was afraid of the man, afraid of his silence and of the ginger moustache and of the supple malacca cane that lay in the glass cupboard in the drawing room.

Lunch over, I left my guardian giving the cook orders, and went to my room.

The window looked out on to the garden path, and a sweeper boy moved up and down the path, a bucket clanging against his naked thighs. He wore only a loincloth, his body was bare and burnt a deep brown, and his head was shaved clean. He went to and from the water tank, and every time he returned to it he bathed, so that his body continually glistened with moisture.

Apart from me, the only boy in the European community of Dehra was this sweeper boy, the low-caste untouchable, the cleaner of pots. But the two of us seldom spoke to each other, one was a servant and the other a sahib and anyway, playing with the sweeper boy would be unhygienic . . . The missionary's wife had said: 'Even if you were an Indian, my child, you would not be allowed to play with the sweeper boy.' So, with whom, then, *could* the sweeper boy play?

The untouchable passed by the window and smiled, but I looked away.

Over the tops of the cherry trees were mountains. Dehra lay in a valley in the foothills, and the small, diminishing European community had its abode on the outskirts of the town.

My guardian's house and the other houses were all built in an English style, with neat front gardens and name-plates on the gates. The surroundings on the whole were so English that people often found it difficult to believe that they did live at the foot of the Himalayas, surrounded by India's thickest jungles. India started a mile away, where the bazaar began.

The bazaar was a fascinating place, and what I had seen of it recently from the window of my guardian's car had been enough to make my heart pound excitely and my imagination soar, but it was a forbidden place—'full of thieves and germs' said the missionary's wife—and I never entered it nowadays save in my dreams.

For Mr Harrison, the missionaries, and their neighbours, this country district of blossoming cherry trees was India. They knew there was a bazaar and a real India not far away, but they did not speak of such places, they chose not to think about them.

The community consisted mostly of elderly people, the others had left soon after Independence. These few stayed because they were too old to start life again in another country, where there would be no servants and very little sunlight; and, though they complained of their lot and criticized the government, they knew their money could buy them their comforts: servants, good food, whisky, almost anything—except the dignity they cherished most . . . .

But Mr Harrison, though he enjoyed the same comforts, remained in the country for different reasons. He did not care who the rulers were so long as they didn't take away his business; he had shares in a number of small tea estates and owned some land—forested land—where, for instance, he hunted deer and wild pig.

I was the only young person in the community, so I was the centre of everyone's attention, particularly the ladies'.

Despite this, I was very lonely.

Every day I walked aimlessly along the road, over the hillside, brooding on the future, or dreaming of sudden and perfect companionship, romance and heroics, hardly ever conscious of the present. When an opportunity for friendship did present itself, as it had the previous day, I simply withdrew into my invisible shell, preferring my own company.

My idle hours were crowded with memories, snatches of childhood. I remembered with fondness my father; he had truly loved me and cared for me, I remembered our long walks and conversations—I missed these so much . . . I had pleasant memories of Grandfather and Grandmother, not so pleasant ones of my mother. At times I wondered about my half-brother . . .

A lot of time now went in studying myself in the dressing-table mirror: I deliberately ignored my pimples and saw instead a grown man, worldly and attractive. Though only seventeen, I felt much older.

Mr John Harrison was going to Delhi.

I intended making the most of his absence: I would squeeze all the freedom I could out of the next few days—explore, get lost, wander afar, even if it were only to find new places to dream in. So I threw myself on the bed and visualized the morrow . . . where should I go—into the hills again, into the forest? Or should I listen to the devil in my heart and go into the bazaar? Tomorrow I would know, tomorrow . . .

❖

The next morning was cold, sharp and fresh. It was quiet until the sun came shooting over the hills, lifting the mist from the valley and clearing the blood-shot from the sky. The ground was wet with dew.

I stood at the gate until my guardian was comfortably seated behind the wheel of the car, and did not move until the car disappeared round the bend in the road.

The missionary's wife, that large, cauliflower-like lady, appeared unexpectedly from behind a hedge and called:

'Good morning, dear! If you aren't very busy this morning, would you like to give me a hand pruning the hedges in my garden?'

The missionary's wife was fond of putting me to work in her garden: if it wasn't cutting the hedge, it was weeding the flower beds and watering the plants, or clearing the garden path of stones, or hunting beetles and ladybirds and dropping them over the wall.

'Oh, good morning,' I stammered. 'Actually, I was going for a walk. Can I help you when I come back, I won't be long . . .'

The missionary's wife looked rather taken aback, for I seldom said no, and before she could make another sally I was on my way. I had a dreadful feeling she would call me back; she was a kind woman, but talkative and boring, and I knew what would follow the garden work: weak tea or lemonade, and then a game of cards, probably beggar-my-neighbour.

But to my relief she called after me: 'All right, dear, come back soon. And be good!'

I waved to her and walked rapidly down the road. And I took a direction different from the one in which I usually wandered.

Far down this road was the bazaar. First I had to pass the rows of neat cottages, and arrive at a commercial area—Dehra's westernized shopping centre, where Europeans, rich Indians, and American tourists en route for Mussoorie could eat at smart restaurants and drink prohibited alcohol. But I had always been afraid and distrustful of anything smart and sophisticated, so I hurried past the shopping centre.

I came to the Clock Tower, which was a tower without a clock. It had been built from public subscriptions, but not enough money had been gathered for the addition of a clock. It had been lifeless five years but served as a good landmark. On the other side of the Clock Tower lay the bazaar, and in the bazaar lay India. On the other side of the Clock Tower began life itself. And all three—the bazaar and India and life itself—were forbidden to me.

My heart raced as I reached the Clock Tower. I was now about to defy the laws of my guardian and of my community. I stood at the Clock Tower, nervous, hesitant, biting my nails. I was afraid of discovery and punishment, but hungering curiosity impelled me forward.

The bazaar and India and life itself all began with a rush of noise and confusion.

A split second of hesitation, and then I plunged into the throng of bustling people; the road was hot and close, alive with the cries of vendors and the smell of cattle and ripening dung. Children played hopscotch in alleyways or gambled with coins, scuffling in the gutter for a lost anna. And the cows moved leisurely through the crowd, nosing around for paper and stale, discarded vegetables; the more daring cows helping themselves at open stalls. And above the uneven tempo of the noise came the blare of a loudspeaker playing a popular piece of music.

I moved along with the crowd, fascinated by the sight of beggars lying on the roadside: naked and emaciated half-humans, some skeletons, some covered with sores; old men dying, children dying, mothers with sucking babies, living and dying. But, strangely enough, I felt nothing for these people; perhaps it was because they were no longer recognizable as humans or because I could not see myself in the same circumstances. And no one else in the bazaar seemed to feel for them.

Like the cows and the loudspeaker, the beggars were a natural growth in the bazaar, and only the well-to-do sacrificing a few annas to placate their consciences were aware of the beggars' presence.

Every little shop was different from the one next to it. After the vegetable stand, green and wet, came the fruit stall; and after the fruit stall, the tea and betel-leaf shop; then the astrologer's platform (Manmohan Mukuldev, B.Astr., foreign degree); and after the astrologer's the toyshop, selling trinkets of gay colours. And then, after the toyshop, another from whose doors poured clouds of smoke.

Curious, I turned to the shop from which the smoke was coming. But I was not the only person making for it. Approaching from the opposite direction was Somi on his bicycle.

Somi, who had not seen me, seemed determined on riding right into the smoky shop on his bicycle; unfortunately his way was blocked by a cow which firmly stood her ground in all the chaos. But the cycle did not lose speed.

I saw the cycle but could only feel sorry for the cow, she was sure to be hurt. But, with the devil in his heart or in the wheels of his machine, Somi swung clear of the animal and collided with me instead—and knocked me into the gutter.

Accustomed as I was to the delicate scents of the missionary's wife's sweet peas and the occasional smell of the bathroom disinfectant, I was nevertheless overpowered by the odour of bad vegetables and kitchen water that rose from the gutter.

'What the hell do you think you're doing?' I cried, choking and spluttering.

'Hullo,' said Somi, gripping me by the arm and helping me up, 'so sorry, not my fault. Anyway, we meet again!'

Anxiously I felt for injuries and, finding none, exclaimed:

'Look at the filthy mess I'm in!'

Somi could not help laughing at my unhappy condition. 'Oh, that is not filth, it is only cabbage water! Do not worry, your clothes will dry . . .' His laugh rang out merrily, and there was something about the laugh, some music in it perhaps, that touched a chord of gaiety in my own heart. Somi was smiling, and on his mouth the smile was friendly and in his soft brown eyes it was mocking.

'Well, I *am* sorry,' said Somi, extending his hand.

I did not take the hand but, looking the other up and down, from turban to slippers, forced myself to say:

'Get out of my way, please.'

'You are a snob,' said Somi without moving. 'You are a very funny one too.'

'I am not a snob,' I retorted involuntarily.

'Then why not forget an accident?'

'You could have missed me, but you didn't try.'

'But if I had missed you, I would have hit the cow! You don't know Maharani—she is the queen of the bazaar cows—if you hurt her she goes mad and smashes half the bazaar! Also, the bicycle might have been spoilt . . . Now please come and have *chaat* with me.'

I had no idea what was meant by the word *chaat,* but before I could refuse the invitation Somi had bundled me into the shop from which the smoke still poured.

At first nothing could be made out; then gradually the smoke seemed to clear and there in front of us, like some shining god, sat a man enveloped in rolls of glistening, oily flesh. In front of him, on a coal fire, was a massive pan in which sizzled a sea of fat, and with deft, practised fingers, he moulded and flipped potato cakes in and out of the pan.

The shop was crowded, but so thick was the screen of smoke and steam, that it was only the murmur of conversation which made known the presence of many people. A plate made of banana leaves was thrust into my hands, and two fried cakes suddenly appeared on it.

'Eat!' said Somi, pressing me down until both of us were seated on the floor, our backs to the wall. 'They are *tikkee*s,' explained Somi, 'tell me if you like them.'

I took a small bite. The *tikkee* was hot. I waited a minute, then tasted another bit. It was still hot but in a different way—now it was lively, interesting; it had a different taste to anything I had eaten before. Suspicious but inquisitive, I finished the *tikkee* and waited to see if anything would happen.

'Have you had this before?' asked Somi.

'No,' I replied anxiously, 'what will it do?'

'It might worry your stomach a little at first, but you will get used to it the more often you eat. So finish the other one too.'

The extent of my submission to Somi's wishes amazed me. At one moment I had been angry, ill-mannered, but, since that laugh of his, I felt like obeying Somi without demur.

He wore a cotton tunic and shorts, and sat cross-legged, his feet pressed against his thighs. His skin was a golden brown, dark on his legs and arms but fair, very fair, where his shirt lay open. His hands were dirty, but eloquent. His eyes, deep brown and dreamy, had depth and roundness.

He said: 'My name is Somi, please tell me what is yours, I have forgotten.'

'Rusty . . .'

'How do you do,' said Somi, 'I am very pleased to meet you, haven't we met before? That was perhaps a long time ago . . . now we are friends, yes, best favourite friends!'

Even though I was a bit peeved by the fact that Somi had forgotten the specifics of our first meeting, I took the warm muddy hand that he offered and shook it. I finished the *tikkee* on my leaf, and accepted another. Then I said: 'How do you do, Somi, I am very pleased to meet you.'

The missionary's wife's head projected itself over the garden wall and broke into a beam of welcome as she spotted me. Hurriedly I returned the smile.

'Where have you been, dear?' asked my garrulous neighbour. 'I was expecting you for lunch. You've never been away so long, I've finished all my work now, you know . . . Was it a nice walk? I know you're thirsty, come in and have a nice cool lemonade, there's nothing like iced lemonade to refresh one after a long walk. I remember when I was a girl, having to walk down to Dehra from Mussoorie, I filled my thermos with lemonade . . .'

I didn't wait to hear the rest of her story—I simply made my escape. I did not wish to hurt the missionary's wife's feelings by refusing the lemonade but, after experiencing the *chaat* shop, the very idea of a lemonade offended me. But I decided that this Sunday I would contribute an extra four annas to the missionary's fund for upkeep of church, wife and garden; and, with this good thought in mind, I went to my room.

The sweeper boy passed by the window, his buckets clanging, his feet going slip-slop on the watery path.

I threw myself on my bed. And now my imagination began building dreams on a newfound reality, for I had agreed to meet Somi again.

And so, the next day, my feet—as if they were acting on their own volition—took me to the *chaat* shop in the bazaar, past the Clock Tower, past the smart shops, down the road, far from my guardian's house.

The fleshy god of the *tikkee*s smiled at me in a manner that seemed to signify that he had recognized in me the potential to become a Regular Customer. The banana plate was ready, the *tikkee*s in it flavoured with spiced sauces.

'Hullo, best favourite friend,' said Somi, appearing out of the surrounding vapour, his slippers loose, chup-chup-chup, loose, open slippers that hung on to the toes by a strap and slapped against the heels as he walked. 'I am glad you came again. After *tikkee*s you must have something else, *chaat* or *gol-guppa*s, all right?'

Somi removed his slippers and joined me—I had somehow managed to sit cross-legged on the ground in the proper fashion.

Somi said, 'Tell me something about yourself. By what misfortune are you an Englishman? How is it that you have been here all your life and never been to a *chaat* shop before?'

'Well, my guardian is very strict,' I said. 'He wants to bring me up in English ways, and he has succeeded . . .'

'Till now,' said Somi, and laughed, the laugh rippling up in his throat, breaking out and forcing its way through the smoke.

Then a large figure loomed in front of us, and I recognized him as Ranbir, the youth I had met on the bicycle.

'Another best favourite friend,' said Somi.

Ranbir did not smile, but opened his mouth a little, gaped at me, and nodded his head. When he nodded, hair fell untidily across his forehead, thick, black, bushy hair, wild and uncontrollable. He wore a long white cotton tunic hanging out over his baggy pyjamas; his feet were bare and dirty; his feet were big and strong.

'Hullo, mister,' said Ranbir, in a gruff voice that disguised his shyness. He said no more for a while, but joined us in our meal.

It was a satisfying fare and I opened up a little as I ate *chaat,* a spicy salad of potato, guava and orange, and then *gol-guppa*s, baked flour cups filled with burning syrups. I felt at ease and began to talk, telling my companions about my school in the hills, the house of my guardian, Mr Harrison himself, and the supple malacca cane. The story was listened to with some amusement: apparently my life had been very dull to date, and Somi and Ranbir pitied me for it.

'Tomorrow is Holi,' said Ranbir, 'you must play with me, then you will be my friend.'

'What is Holi?' I asked.

Ranbir looked at me in amazement. 'You do not know about Holi! It is the Hindu Festival of Colour! It is the day on which we celebrate the coming of spring, when we throw colour on each other and shout and sing and forget our misery, for the colours mean the rebirth of spring and a new life in our hearts . . . You do not know of it!'

I was somewhat bewildered by Ranbir's sudden eloquence, and began to have doubts about this game; it seemed to me a primitive sort of pastime, this throwing of paint about the place.

'I might get into trouble,' I said rather uncertainly. 'I'm not supposed to come here, anyway, and my guardian might return any day . . .'

'Don't tell him about it,' said Ranbir.

'Oh, he has ways of finding out. I'll get a thrashing.'

'Huh!' said Ranbir, a disappointed and somewhat disgusted expression on his mobile face. 'You are afraid of spoiling your clothes, mister, that is it. You are just a snob.'

Somi laughed. 'That's what I told him yesterday, and only then did he join me in the *chaat* shop. I think we should call him a snob whenever he makes excuses.' Meanwhile, I was enjoying the *chaat*. I ate *gol-guppa* after *gol-guppa*, until my throat was almost aflame and my stomach burning itself out. I was not very concerned about Holi. I was content with the present, content to enjoy the newfound pleasures of the *chaat* shop, and said:

'Well I'll see . . . If my guardian doesn't come back tomorrow, I'll play Holi with you, all right?'

Ranbir was pleased. He said, 'I will be waiting in the jungle behind your house. When you hear the drumbeat in the jungle, understand that I am waiting for you. Then come.'

'Will you be there too, Somi?' I asked. Somehow, I felt safe in Somi's presence.

'I do not play Holi,' said Somi. 'You see, I am different from Ranbir. I wear a turban and he does not, also there is a bangle on my wrist, which means that I am a Sikh. We don't play Holi. But I will see you the day after, here in the *chaat* shop.'

Somi left the shop, and was swallowed up by smoke and steam, but the chup-chup of his loose slippers could be heard for some time, until their sound was lost in the greater sound of the bazaar outside.

In the bazaar, people haggled over counters, children played in the spring sunshine, dogs courted one another, and Ranbir and I continued eating *gol-guppas*.

The afternoon was warm and lazy, unusually so for spring, very quiet, as though resting in the interval between the spring and the coming summer. There was no sign of the missionary's wife or the sweeper boy when I returned, but Mr Harrison's car stood in the driveway of the house.

At that sight of the car, I felt a little weak and frightened; I had not expected my guardian to return so soon and had, in fact, almost forgotten his existence. But now I forgot all about the *chaat* shop and Somi and Ranbir, and ran up the veranda steps in panic.

Mr Harrison was at the top of the veranda steps, standing behind the potted palms.

'Oh, hullo, sir, you're back!' I exclaimed, trying to make my little piece sound enthusiastic as I knew of nothing else to say.

'Where have you been all day?' asked Mr Harrison, without even looking at me. 'Our neighbours haven't seen much of you lately.'

I was startled. So he had already been informed . . . no doubt, it was the missionary's wife who was forever gossiping. I had to lie—had to prevent Mr Harrison from finding out the truth.

'I've been for a walk, sir.'

'You have been to the bazaar.'

I hesitated before making a denial; his eyes were on me now, and to lie I would have had to lower my eyes—and this I could not do . . .

'Yes, sir, I went to the bazaar.'

'May I ask why?'

'Because I had nothing to do.'

'If you had nothing to do, you could have visited our neighbours. The bazaar is not the place for you. You know that.'

'But nothing happened to me . . .'

'That is not the point,' said Mr Harrison, and now his normally dry voice took on a faint shrill note of excitement, and he spoke rapidly. 'The point is, I have told you never to visit the bazaar. You belong here, to this house, this road, these people. Don't go where you don't belong.'

I wanted to argue, longed to rebel, but fear of Mr Harrison held me back. I wanted to resist the man's authority, but I was conscious of the supple malacca cane in the glass cupboard.

'I'm sorry, sir . . .'

But my cowardice did me no good. Mr Harrison

went over to the glass cupboard, brought out the cane and flexed it in his hands. He said:

'It is not enough to say you are sorry, you must be made to feel sorry. Bend over the sofa.' I bent over the sofa, clenched my teeth and dug my fingers into the cushions. The cane swished through the air, landing on my bottom with a slap, knocking the dust from my pants. I felt no pain. But my guardian waited, allowing the cut to sink in, then he administered the second stroke, and this time it hurt, it stung into my buttocks, burning up the flesh, conditioning it for the remaining cuts.

At the sixth stroke of the supple malacca cane, which was usually the last, a wild whoop escaped involuntarily from my throat, and I leapt over the sofa and charged from the room.

I lay on my bed groaning until the pain had eased.

But the flesh was so sore that I could not touch the place where the cane had fallen. Wriggling out of my pants, I examined my backside in the mirror. Mr Harrison had been most accurate: a thick purple welt stretched across both cheeks, and a little blood trickled down my thigh. The blood had a cool, almost soothing effect, but the sight of it made me feel faint.

I lay down and moaned for pleasure. I indulged in so much self-pity that I felt like crying but I knew the futility of tears. Nevertheless, the pain and the sense of injustice I felt were both real.

A shadow fell across the bed. Someone was at the window, and I looked up.

The sweeper boy showed his teeth.

'What do you want?' I asked gruffly.

'You hurt, *chotta sahib*?'

The sweeper boy's sympathies provoked only suspicion in me.

'You told Mr Harrison where I went!' I said accusingly. I was so furious with him. But the sweeper boy cocked his head to one side, and asked innocently, 'Where you went, *chotta sahib*?'

'Oh, never mind. Go away.'

'But you hurt?'

'Get out!' I shouted.

The smile vanished, leaving only a sad, frightened look in the sweeper boy's eyes.

I hated hurting people's feelings, but I was not accustomed to the sweeper boy, and yet, only a few minutes ago, I had been beaten for visiting the bazaar where there were so many like the sweeper boy.

The sweeper boy turned from the window, leaving wet finger-marks on the sill, then lifted his buckets from the ground and, with his knees bent to take the weight, walked away. His feet splashed a little in the water he had spilt, and the soft red mud flew up and flecked his legs.

Angry with my guardian and with the servant and most of all with myself, I buried my head in my pillow and tried to shut out reality; I fabricated a wonderful dream, in which I was thrashing Mr Harrison until he begged me for mercy.

I woke to the sound of drumbeats, and lay in bed and listened; it was repeated, travelling over the still air and in through the bedroom window. *Dhum!* . . . A double-beat now, one deep, one high, insistent, questioning . . . It was still dark, dawn was yet to come. I remembered my promise, that I would play Holi with Ranbir, meet him in the jungle when he beat the drum. But I had made the promise on the condition that my guardian did not return; I could not possibly keep it now, not after the thrashing I had received.

Dhum-dhum, spoke the drum in the forest, *dhum-dhum,* impatient and getting annoyed . . .

'Why can't he shut up,' I wondered with annoyance, 'does he want to wake Mr Harrison . . .'

Holi, the Festival of Colours, the arrival of spring, the rebirth of the new year, the awakening of love, of what importance were these things to me? They did not concern my life. I could not start a new life, not for one day . . . besides, it all sounded very primitive, this throwing of colour and beating of drums . . .

Dhum-dhum!

I sat up in bed.

The sky had grown lighter.

From the distant bazaar came a new music, many drums and voices, faint but steady, growing in rhythm and excitement. I felt as if that sound was conveying something to me . . . something wild and emotional, something that belonged to my dream world, and on a sudden impulse I sprang out of bed.

I went to the door and listened; the house was quiet. I bolted the door. The colours of Holi, I knew, would stain my clothes, so I did not remove my pyjamas. In an old pair of flattened rubber-soled tennis shoes, I climbed out of the window and ran over the dew-wet grass, down the path behind the house, over the hill and into the jungle.

When Ranbir saw me approach, he rose from the ground. The long hand-drum, the *dholak*, hung at his waist. As he rose, the sun rose. But the sun did not look as fiery as Ranbir who appeared as a painted demon. His thick mass of hair was covered with red dust and his body, naked but for a cloth round his waist, was smeared green; he looked like a painted demon, a green demon.

'You are late, mister,' said Ranbir, 'I thought you were not coming.'

He had both his fists closed, but when he walked towards me he opened them, smiling widely, a white smile in a green face. In his right hand was red dust and in his left hand green dust. And with his right hand he rubbed the red dust on my left cheek, and then with the other hand he put the green dust on my right cheek; then he stood back and looked at me and laughed. Then he embraced me. Seeing my bewildered expression, he told me that it was local custom to embrace on Holi. It was a wrestler's hug, and I winced breathlessly.

'Come,' said Ranbir, 'let us go and paint the town in the colours of a rainbow.'

And truly, that day there was an outbreak of spring.

The sun came up, and the bazaar woke up. The walls of the houses were suddenly patched with splashes of colour, and just as suddenly the trees seemed to have burst into flower, for in the forest there were armies of rhododendrons, and by the river the poinsettias danced; the cherry and the plum were in blossom; the snow in the mountains had melted, and the streams were rushing down in torrents; the new leaves on the trees were full of sweetness, and the young grass held both dew and sun, making an emerald of every dewdrop.

The infection of spring spread simultaneously through the world of man and the world of nature, and made them one.

Ranbir and I moved round the hill, keeping in the fringe of the jungle until we had skirted not only the European community but also the smart shopping centre. We came down dirty little side streets where the walls of houses, stained with the wear and tear of many years of meagre habitation, were now stained again with the vivid colours of Holi. Then we came to the Clock Tower.

At the Clock Tower, spring had really been declared open. Clouds of coloured dust rose in the air and spread, and jets of water—green and orange and purple, all rich and vibrant colours—burst out everywhere.

Children played in groups and were armed mainly with bicycle pumps, or pumps fashioned from bamboo stems, from which was squirted coloured water. And the children paraded the main road, chanting shrilly and clapping their hands. Adults preferred the dust to the water. They too sang, but their chanting held a significance, their hands and fingers drummed the rhythms of spring, the same rhythms, the same songs that belonged to this day every year of their lives.

Ranbir was met by some friends and greeted with great hilarity. Before I could realize what was happening a bicycle pump was directed at me and a jet of sooty black water squirted on my face.

Blinded for a moment, I blundered about in great confusion. A horde of children bore down on me, and I was subjected to a pumping from all sides. My shirt and pyjamas, drenched through, stuck to my skin; then someone gripped the end of my shirt and tugged at it until it tore and came away. Dust was thrown on my face and body, roughly and with full force, and my skin—tender and underexposed—smarted beneath the onslaught.

Then my eyes cleared. I blinked and looked wildly round at the group of boys and girls who cheered and danced in front of me. My body was running mostly with sooty black, streaked with red, and my mouth seemed full of it too, and I began to spit.

Then, one by one, Ranbir's friends approached me.

Gently, they rubbed dust on my cheeks, and embraced me; they were like so many flaming demons that I could not distinguish one from the other. But this gentle greeting coming so soon after the stormy bicycle-pump attack, bewildered me even more.

Ranbir said: 'Now you are one of us, Rusty, come,' and I went with him and the others.

'Suri is hiding,' cried someone. 'He has locked himself in his house and won't play Holi!'

'Well, he will have to play,' said Ranbir, 'even if we break the house down.'

We knocked on the door of Suri's house. His mother answered the door and told us that Suri, who dreaded Holi, had decided to spend the day in a state of siege. He had set up camp in the kitchen, where there were provisions enough for the whole day. We then went to that side of the courtyard and yelled out at him. He listened to us calling to him, and ignored our invitations, jeers and threats; the door was strong and well-barricaded so he must have happily thought that he was safe. But we were too intoxicated by the drumming and shouting and high spirits to be done out of the pleasure of discomfiting Suri. So we acquired a ladder and made our entry into the kitchen by the skylight. There we saw Suri settled beneath a table, going through a English nudists' journal. We yelled at him. Suri squealed with fright. The door was opened and he was bundled out, and his spectacles were trampled upon.

'My glasses!' he screamed. 'You've broken them!'

'You can afford a dozen pairs!' jeered someone in our group.

'But I can't see, you fools, I can't see!'

'He can't see!' cried someone else in scorn. 'For once in his life, Suri can't see what's going on! Now, whenever he spies, we'll smash his glasses!'

Not knowing Suri all that well, I could not help pitying the frantic boy.

'Why don't you let him go,' I asked Ranbir. 'Don't force him if he doesn't want to play.'

'But this is the only chance we have of repaying him for all his dirty tricks. It is the only day on which no one needs to be afraid of him!'

I could not imagine how anyone could possibly be afraid of this pale, struggling, spindly-legged boy who was almost being torn apart, and was glad when the others had finished their sport with him.

All day I roamed the town and countryside with Ranbir and his friends, and Suri was soon forgotten. For one day, Ranbir and his friends forgot their homes and their work, and danced down the roads, out of the town and into the forest. And, for one day, I forgot my guardian and the missionary's wife and the supple malacca cane, and ran along joyously with the others.

The crisp, sunny morning ripened into afternoon.

In the forest, in the cool dark silence of the jungle, everyone stopped singing and shouting, suddenly exhausted. We lay down in the shade of many trees, and the grass was soft and comfortable, and very soon most of us were fast asleep.

But sleep evaded me. I was tired. And hungry. I had lost my shirt and shoes, my feet were bruised, my body sore. It was only now, resting, that I noticed these things, for I had been so far caught up in the excitement of the colour game, overcome by an exhilaration I had never known. My hair was tousled and streaked with colour.

I was exhausted, but I felt happy.

I wanted this to go on for ever, this day of feverish emotion, this life in another world. I did not want to leave the forest; it was safe, its earth soothed me, gathered me in, so that the pain of my body became a pleasure . . .

No, I did not want to go home.

Mr Harrison stood at the top of the veranda steps. The house was in darkness, but his cigarette glowed more brightly for it. A road lamp cast light on me as I opened the gate. I knew I had been spotted, but I didn't care much; but if I had known then that Mr Harrison had not recognized me, I would have turned back instead of walking resignedly up the garden path.

Mr Harrison did not move, nor did he appear to notice my approach. It was only when I started up the veranda steps that he moved and said:

'Who's that?'

Obviously he had not recognized me; I wished that I realized this earlier for in that instant I became aware of my own condition, for my body was a patchwork of paint. Wearing only torn pyjamas I could, in the half-light, have easily been mistaken for the sweeper boy or someone else's servant. It must have been a newly-acquired bazaar-instinct that made me think of escape. I turned about.

But Mr Harrison shouted, 'Come here, you!' and the tone of his voice—the tone reserved for the sweeper boy—stopped me in my tracks.

'Come up here!' repeated Mr Harrison.

I returned to the veranda, and my guardian switched on a light, but even now there was no recognition.

'Good evening, sir,' I said as calmly as I could.

Mr Harrison received a shock. I felt like laughing out loud, but I know what he must have gone through: anger and then pain. As soon as he recovered from that shock he began to fire me. 'Are you the same Rusty I trained and educated? No, you are just a wild, ragged, ungrateful wretch who does not know the difference between what is proper and what is improper, what is civilized and what is barbaric, what is decent and what is shameful! All my years of training have come to nothing.' He then came out of the shadows and cursed. He brought his hand down on the back of my neck, propelled me into the drawing room, and pushed me across the room so violently that I lost my balance, collided with a table and rolled over on to the ground.

I looked up from the floor to find my guardian standing over me, and in his right hand was the supple malacca cane, and the cane was twitching.

Mr Harrison's face was twitching too; it was full of fire. His lips were stitched together, sealed up with the ginger moustache, and he looked at me with narrowed, unblinking eyes full of contempt.

'Filth!' he said, almost spitting the words in my face. 'My God, what filth!'

I don't know what came over me—instead of begging for mercy I simply stood and stared, fascinated by the deep yellow nicotine stains on the fingers of my guardian's raised hand. Then the wrist moved suddenly and the cane cut across my face like a knife, stabbing and burning into my cheek.

I cried out and cowered back against the wall; I could feel the blood trickling across my mouth. I looked round desperately for a means of escape, but Mr Harrison was in front of me, over me, and the wall was behind.

Mr Harrison broke into a torrent of words once again. 'How can you call yourself an Englishman? How can you come back to this house in such a condition? In what gutter, in what brothel have you been! Have you seen yourself? Do you know what you look like?'

'No,' I replied. For the first time I did not address my guardian as 'sir'. 'I don't care what I look like.'

'You don't! . . . Well, I'll tell you what you look like! You look like the native that you are!'

'That's a lie!' I exclaimed, outraged more by his tone than by his words.

'It's the truth. I've tried to bring you up as an Englishman, as your father would have wished. But, as you won't have it our way, I'm telling you that your parentage is just about the only thing English about you. You're no better than the sweeper boy!'

I flared into a temper and showed some spirit in front of that man for the first time in my life. 'I'm no better than the sweeper boy, but I'm as good as him! I'm as good as you! I'm as good as anyone!' And, instead of cringing to take the cut from the cane, I flung myself at my guardian's legs. The cane swished through the air, grazing my back. But I was beyond caring. I wrapped my arms round my guardian's legs and pulled on them with all my strength.

Mr Harrison went over, falling flat on his back. The suddenness of the fall must have knocked the breath from his body, because for a moment he did not move.

I sprang to my feet. The cut across my face had stung me to madness, to an unreasoning hate, and I then did what previously I would only have dreamt of doing. Lifting a vase of the missionary's wife's best sweet peas off the glass cupboard, I flung it at Mr Harrison's face. It hit him on the chest, but the water and flowers flopped out over his face. He tried to get up, but he was speechless.

The look of alarm on Mr Harrison's face gave me greater courage. Before the man could recover his feet and his balance, I gripped him by the collar and pushed him backwards, until both of us fell over on to the floor. With one hand still twisting his collar, I slapped my guardian's face. Mad with the pain in my own face, I hit the man again and again, wildly and awkwardly, but with the giddy thrill of knowing I could do it: I was a child no longer, I was seventeen, I was a man. I could inflict pain, that was a wonderful discovery; there was a power in my body—a devil or a god—and I gained confidence in my power.

'Stop that, stop it!'

The shout of a hysterical woman brought me to my senses. I still held my guardian by the throat, but I stopped hitting him. Mr Harrison's face was very red.

The missionary's wife stood in the doorway, her face white with fear. She was perhaps under the impression that Mr Harrison was being attacked by a servant or some bazaar hooligan. I did not wait for her to recognize me, so before she even found her tongue I darted out of the drawing room with a newfound speed and agility.

I made my escape through the bedroom window. From the gate I could see the missionary's wife silhouetted against the drawing-room light. I laughed out loud. The woman swivelled round and came forward a few steps. And I laughed again and began running down the road to the bazaar.

It was late. The sweet shops and restaurants were closed. In the bazaar, oil lamps hung outside each doorway; people were asleep on the steps and platforms of shopfronts, some huddled in blankets, others rolled tight into themselves. The road, which during the day was a busy, noisy crush of people and animals, was quiet and deserted. Only a lean dog still sniffed in the gutter. A woman sang in a room high above the street—a plaintive, tremulous song—and in the far distance a jackal cried to the moon. But the empty, lifeless street was very deceptive; if the roofs could have been removed from but a handful of buildings, it would be seen that life had not really stopped but, beautiful and ugly, persisted through the night.

It was past midnight, though the Clock Tower had no way of saying it. I was in the empty street, and the *chaat* shop was closed, a sheet of tarpaulin draped across the front. I looked up and down the road, hoping to meet someone I knew: the *chaat-wallah*, I felt sure, would give me a blanket for the night and a place to sleep; and the next day when Somi came to meet me, I would tell my friend of my predicament, that I had run away from my guardian's house and did not intend returning. But I would have to wait till morning: the *chaat* shop was shuttered, barred and bolted.

I sat down on the steps, but the stone was cold and my thin cotton pyjamas offered no protection. I folded my arms and huddled up in a corner, but still I shivered. My feet were becoming numb, lifeless.

The hazards of the situation had not yet sunk into me. I was still mad with anger and rebellion and though the blood on my cheek had dried, my face was still smarting. I could not think clearly: the present seemed confusing and unreal and I could not see beyond it; what worried me in fact was the cold and the discomfort and the pain.

The singing stopped in the high window. I looked up and saw a beckoning hand. As no one else in the street showed any signs of life, I got up and walked across the road until I was under the window. The woman pointed to a stairway, and I mounted it, glad of the hospitality I was being offered.

The stairway seemed to go to the stars, but it turned suddenly to lead into the woman's room. The door was slightly ajar. I knocked and a voice said, 'Come . . .'

The room was filled with perfume and burning

incense. A musical instrument lay in one corner. The woman reclined on a bed, her hair scattered about the pillow; she had a round, pretty face, but she was losing her youth, and the fat showed in rolls at her exposed waist. She smiled at me, and beckoned again.

'Thank you,' I said, closing the door. 'Can I sleep here?'

'Where else?' said the woman.

'Just for tonight.'

She smiled, and waited. I just stood in front of her, my hands behind my back.

'Sit down,' she said, and patted the bedclothes beside her.

Reverently, and as respectfully as was possible, I sat down. The woman ran little fair fingers over my body, and drew my head to hers; our lips were very close, almost touching. I thought that our breathing sounded terribly loud, but I only said:

'I am hungry.'

In reply, the woman kissed me full on the lips. I drew away in embarrassment, unsure of myself. I liked this woman, but for some inexplicable reason her behaviour worried me . . .

'What is wrong?' she asked.

'I'm tired,' I said.

The friendly smile on her face turned to a look of

scorn. Then she must have seen the unhappiness in my eyes, for in a voice full of kindness she said, 'You can sleep here until you have lost your tiredness.'

But now I didn't want to remain in that room any longer—it didn't seem right. I shook my head. 'I will come some other time,' I said, not wishing to hurt her feelings.

I left the room not knowing what prompted my actions. Mechanically, I descended the staircase, and walked up the bazaar road, past the silent, sleeping forms, until I reached the Clock Tower. To the right of the Clock Tower was a broad stretch of grassland where, during the day, cattle grazed and children played and young men like Ranbir wrestled and kicked footballs. But now, at night, it was a vast empty space.

The grass was soft, like the grass in the forest, and I walked the length of the *maidan*. I found a bench and sat down, warmer for the walk. A light breeze was blowing across the *maidan*, pleasant and refreshing, playing with my hair. Around me everything was dark and silent and lonely. I had got away from the bazaar, which held the misery of beggars and homeless children and starving dogs, and I could now concentrate on my own misery, for nothing made me unhappier than my own lonely state. Madness and freedom and violence were new to me: loneliness was familiar, something I understood.

I was alone. Until tomorrow, I was alone for the rest of my life.

If tomorrow there was no Somi at the *chaat* shop, no Ranbir, then what would I do? This question badgered me persistently, making me an unwilling slave to reality. I did not know where these friends of mine lived, I had no money, I could not ask the *chaat-wallah* for credit on the strength of two visits. Perhaps I would return to the amorous lady in the bazaar, perhaps . . . but no, one thing was certain, I would never return to my guardian . . .

The moon had been hidden by clouds, and presently there was a drizzle. I did not mind the rain, it refreshed me and made the colour run from my body; but, when it began to fall harder, I started shivering again. I felt sick. I got up, rolled my ragged pyjamas up to my thighs and crawled under the bench.

There was a hollow under the bench, and at first I found it quite comfortable. But there was no grass and gradually the earth began to soften: soon I was on my hands and knees in a pool of muddy water, with the slush oozing up through my fingers and toes. Crouching there, wet and cold and muddy, I was overcome by a feeling of helplessness and self-pity: everyone and everything seemed to have turned against me, not only my people, but also the bazaar and the *chaat* shop and even the elements. I admitted to myself rather grudgingly that I had been too impulsive in rebelling and running away from home; perhaps there was still time to return and beg Mr Harrison's forgiveness. But could my behaviour be forgiven? I may be clapped in irons for attempted murder. Most certainly I would be given another beating: not six strokes this time, but nine.

My only hope was Somi. If not Somi, then Ranbir. If not Ranbir . . . well, it was no use thinking further, there was no one else to think of.

The rain had ceased. I crawled out from under the bench, and stretched my cramped limbs. The moon came out from a cloud, and played on my wet, glistening body, and showed me the vast, naked loneliness of the *maidan* and my own insignificance. I longed now for the presence of people, be they beggars or women, and I broke into a trot, and the trot became a run, a frightened run. I did not stop until I reached the Clock Tower.

My weariness coupled with hunger and pain was so great that even long after the sun had come striding down the road, knocking on nearly every door and window, I was still asleep on the steps of the *chaat*

shop. Someone shook me by my shoulders and woke me up. It was Somi. 'Hey, Rusty, get up, what has happened? Where is Ranbir? Holi got over yesterday, you know! Anyway, by the time you rouse yourself, let me take my bath.'

Somi went a little ahead and bathed at the common water tank. He stood under the tap and slapped his body into life and spluttered with the shock of mountain water.

At the tank were many people: children shrieking with delight—or discomfort—as their *ayah*s slapped them about roughly and affectionately; the *ayah*s themselves, strong, healthy hill-women, with heavy bracelets on their ankles; the *bhisti*—water-carrier—with his skin bag; and the cook with his pots and pans. The *ayah*s sat on their haunches, bathing the children, their saris rolled up to the thighs; every time they moved their feet, the bells on their anklets jingled, so that there was a continuous shrieking and jingling and slapping of buttocks. The cook smeared his utensils with ash and washed them, and filled an earthen *chatty* with water; the *bhisti* hoisted the water-bag over his shoulder and left, dripping; a piedog lapped at water rolling off the stone platform; and a baleful-looking cow nibbled at wet grass.

Obviously, it was with these people that Somi spent his mornings, laughing and talking and bathing with

them. When he had finished his ablutions, dried his hair in the sun, dressed and tied his turban, he walked up to me, and seeing me lying there with my eyes open he said, 'Hey, your guardian will be very angry!'

I sat up with a start. I was wide awake now, sweeping up my scattered thoughts and sorting them out. It was difficult for me to be straightforward, but I forced myself to look Somi straight in the eyes and, very simply and without preamble, said:

'I've run away from home.'

Somi showed no surprise. A half-smile on his lips, he said:

'Good. Now you can come and stay with me.' Oh, what a relief to hear those words! I felt weak in the legs, but my mind was at ease and I no longer felt alone: once again, Somi gave me a feeling of confidence. We headed for Somi's house on his bicycle.

'Do you think I can get a job?' I asked.

'Don't worry about that yet, you have only just run away.'

'Do you think I can get a job?' I asked again. If I didn't get a job, how would I live?

'Why not? But don't worry, you are going to stay with me.'

'I'll stay with you only until I find a job. Any kind of job, there must be something.'

'Of course, don't worry,' said Somi, and pressed harder on the pedals.

We came to a canal; it was noisy with the rush of mountain water, for the snows had begun to melt. The road, which ran parallel to the canal, was flooded in some parts, but Somi steered a steady course. Then the canal turned left and the road kept straight, and presently the sound of water was but a murmur, and the road quiet and shady; there were trees at the road-sides, covered in pink and white blossoms, and behind them more trees, thicker and greener, and amongst the trees were houses.

A boy swung on a creaking wooden gate. He whistled out, and Somi waved back; that was all. 'Who's that?' I asked.

'Son of his parents.'

'What do you mean by that?'

'His father is rich. So Kishen is somebody. He has money, and it is as powerful as Suri's tongue.'

'Is he Suri's friend or yours?'

'When it suits him, he is our friend. When it suits him, he is Suri's friend.'

'Then he's clever as well as rich,' I deduced.

'The brains are his mother's.'

'And the money his father's?'

'Yes, but there isn't much left now. Mr Kapoor

is finished . . . Kishen looks like his father too, his mother is beautiful. Well, here we are!'

Somi rode the bicycle in amongst the trees and along a snaky path that dodged this way and that, and then we reached his house.

It was a small flat house, covered completely by a crimson bougainvillaea creeper. The garden was a mass of marigolds, which had sprung up everywhere, even in the cracks at the sides of the veranda steps. No one was at home. Somi's father was in Delhi, and his mother was out for the morning, buying the week's vegetables.

'Have you any brothers?' I asked, as we entered the front room.

'No. But I've got two sisters. But they're married. Come on, let's see if my clothes will fit you.' I laughed, for I was older and bigger than my friend, and I was used to wearing shirts and trousers. I sat down on a sofa in the front room, whilst Somi went for the clothes.

The room was cool and spacious, and had very little furniture. But on the walls were many pictures, and in the centre a large one of Guru Nanak, the founder of the Sikh religion; his body bare, the saint sat with his legs crossed and the palms of his hands touching in prayer, and on his face there was a serene expression: the serenity of Nanak's countenance seemed to communicate itself to the room. There was a serenity about Somi too, maybe because of the smile that always hovered near his mouth.

Somi's family appeared to be middle-class people; that is, they were neither rich nor beggars, but managed to live all the same.

Somi came back with the clothes.

'They are mine,' he said, 'so maybe they will be a little small for you. Anyway, the warm weather is coming and it will not matter what you wear—better nothing at all!'

I put on a long white shirt which, to my surprise, hung loose; it had a high collar and broad sleeves.

'It is loose,' I said wonderingly, 'how can it be yours?'

'It is made loose,' said Somi.

I pulled on a pair of white pyjamas, and these were definitely small for me, ending a few inches above the ankle. The sandals would not buckle; so, when I walked, they behaved like Somi's and slapped against my heels.

'There!' exclaimed Somi in satisfaction. 'Now everything is settled, *chaat* in your stomach, clean clothes on your body, and in a few days we find a job! Now is there anything else?'

I knew Somi well enough now to know that it wasn't necessary to thank him for anything. Gratitude was taken for granted; in true friendship there are no formalities and no obligations. I did not even ask him if he had consulted his mother about taking me in as a guest; perhaps she was used to this sort of thing.

'Is there anything else?' repeated Somi.

A small yawn escaped me.

'Can I go to sleep now, please?'

I had never slept well in my guardian's house, because I had never been tired enough; also, my imagination often disturbed me. And, since running away, I had slept very badly, because I had been cold and hungry and afraid. But in Somi's house I felt safe and a little happy, and so I slept; in fact I slept through the rest of the day and through the night.

In the morning Somi tipped me out of bed and dragged me to the water tank. I watched him strip and stand under the jet of tap water, and shuddered at the prospect of having to do the same.

Before removing my shirt, I looked around in embarrassment; no one paid much attention to me, though one of the *ayahs,* a girl with bangles, gave me a sly smile. I looked away from the women, threw my shirt on a bush and advanced cautiously to the bathing place.

Somi pulled me under the tap. I gasped with shock at the icy-cold water and sprang off the platform, much to the amusement of everyone present.

There was no towel with which to dry myself so I stood on the grass, shivering with cold, wondering whether I should dash back to the house or shiver in the open until the sun dried me. But the girl with the bangles was beside me holding a towel. Her eyes were full of mockery, but her smile was friendly.

At the midday meal, which consisted of curry and curds and *chapattis*, I met Somi's mother. I liked her quite a bit.

She was a woman of about thirty-five; she had a few grey hairs at the temples, and her skin—unlike Somi's—was rough and dry. She was dressed simply, in a plain white sari. Her life had been difficult. During the partition of the country, when hate made religion its own, Somi's family had to leave their home in the Punjab and trek southwards; they had walked hundreds of miles. Life had to be started again right from the beginning, for they had lost most of their property: Somi's father found work in Delhi, his sister was married off, and Somi and his mother settled down in Dehra, where Somi attended school.

His mother said: 'Mister Rusty, you must give Somi a few lessons in spelling and arithmetic. Always, he comes last in class.'

'Oh, that's good!' exclaimed Somi. 'We'll have fun, Rusty!' Then he thumped the table. 'I have an idea! I think I have a job for you! Remember Kishen, the boy we passed yesterday? Well, his father wants someone to give him private lessons in English.'

'Teach Kishen?'

'Yes, it will be easy. I'll go and see Mr Kapoor and tell him that I've found a professor of English or something like that, and then you can come and see him. Brother, it is a first-class idea, you are going to be a teacher!'

I felt very dubious about the proposal; I wasn't sure I could teach English or anything else to the wilful son of a rich man, but I wasn't in a position to pick and choose. Somi mounted his bicycle and rode off to see Mr Kapoor about the job. When he returned he seemed pleased with himself, and my heart sank with the knowledge that I had got a job.

'You are to come and see him this evening,' announced Somi, 'he will tell you all about it. They want a teacher for Kishen, especially if they don't have to pay.'

'What kind of a job is this—without pay?' I complained.

'No pay,' said Somi, 'but everything else—food and a room, sir!'

'Oh, even a room,' I muttered, a trifle ungratefully, 'that will be nice.'

'Anyway,' said Somi, 'go and see him, you don't have to accept the job right away.'

The house the Kapoors lived in was very near the canal; it was a squat, comfortable-looking bungalow, surrounded by uncut hedges, and shaded by banana and papaya trees. It was late evening when Somi and I arrived; the moon was up, and the shaggy branches of the banana trees shook their heavy shadows out over the gravel path.

In an open space in front of the house a log fire was burning; the Kapoors appeared to be throwing a party. We joined a group of people who were standing round the fire, and I wondered if Somi and I had been invited to the party. The fire lent a friendly warmth to the chilly night, and the flames leapt up, casting the glow of roses on people's faces.

Somi pointed out different people: various shopkeepers, one or two 'Big Men', the sickly-looking Suri (who was never absent from a social occasion such as this) and a few total strangers who had invited themselves to the party just for the fun of the thing and a free meal. Kishen, the Kapoors' son, was not present; apparently he hated parties, preferring the company of certain wild friends in the bazaar.

Apparently, Mr Kapoor was once a 'Big Man' himself, and everyone knew this, but he had fallen from the heights, and until he gave up the bottle, was not likely to reach them again. Everyone felt sorry for his wife, including herself.

Presently Kapoor tottered out of the front door arm-in-arm with a glass and a bottle of whisky. He wore a green dressing-gown and a week's beard; his hair, or what was left of it, stood up on end; and he dribbled slightly. An awkward silence fell on the company, but Kapoor, who was a friendly, gentle sort of drunkard, looked round benevolently, and said:

'Everybody here? Fine, fine, they are all here, all of them . . . Throw some more wood on the fire!' The fire was doing very well indeed, but not well enough for Kapoor; every now and then he would throw a log on the flames until it was feared the blaze would reach the house. Meena, Kapoor's wife, did not look flustered, only irritated; she was a capable person, still young, a charming hostess, and, in her red sari and white silk jacket, her hair plaited and scented with jasmine, she looked beautiful. I could not help gazing admiringly at her. I wanted to compliment her, to say 'Mrs Kapoor, you are beautiful', but I had no need to tell her, she appeared to be fully conscious of the fact.

Meena Kapoor made her way over to one of the 'Big Men', and whispered something in his ear, and then she went to a 'Little Shopkeeper' and whispered something in his ear, and then both the 'Big Man' and the 'Little Shopkeeper' advanced stealthily towards the spot where Mr Kapoor was holding forth, and made a gentle attempt to convey him indoors.

But Kapoor was having none of it. He pushed the men aside and roared:

'Keep the fire burning! Keep it burning, don't let it go out, throw some more wood on it!'

And before he could be restrained, he threw a pot of the most delicious sweetmeats on to the flames.

I found this absolutely sacrilegous. 'Oh, Mr Kapoor . . .' I cried out, but there was some confusion in the rear, and my words were drowned in a series of explosions.

Suri, with one or two others, had begun letting off fireworks: fountains, rockets and explosives. The fountains gushed forth in green and red and silver lights, and the rockets struck through the night with crimson tails, but it was the explosives that caused the confusion. The guests did not know whether to press forward into the fires, or retreat amongst the fireworks; neither prospect was pleasing, and the women began to show signs of hysterics. Then Suri burnt his finger and began screaming, and this distraction was what all the women needed. Headed by Suri's mother, they rushed to the boy and smothered him with attention, whilst the men, who were in a minority, looked on sheepishly as if they wished that the accident had been of a more serious nature.

Something rough brushed against my cheek. It was Kapoor's beard. Somi had brought our host to me, and the bemused man put his face close to mine and placed his hands on my shoulders in order to steady himself. He nodded his head, his eyes red and watery.

'Rusty . . . so you are Mister Rusty . . . I hear you are going to be my school teacher.'

'Your son's, sir,' I corrected him, 'but that is for you to decide.'

'Do not call me "sir",' he said, wagging his finger in my face, 'call me by my name. So you are going to England, eh?'

'No, I'm going to be your school teacher.' I couldn't help being sarcastic. I don't think I've ever had patience for people who drink themselves silly and make fools of themselves. I had to put my arm round Kapoor's waist to avoid being dragged to the ground; Kapoor was leaning heavily on my shoulders.

'Good, good. Tell me after you have gone, I want to give you some addresses of people I know. You must go to Monte Carlo. You've seen nothing until you've seen Monte Carlo, it's the only place with a future . . . Who built Monte Carlo, do you know?'

Naturally it was impossible for me to make any sense of such a conversation or discuss my appointment as Professor in English to Kishen Kapoor. Kapoor meanwhile began to slip from my arms, and I took the opportunity of changing my own position for a more comfortable one, before levering my host up again. The amused smiles of the company rested on this little scene.

I asked the question which Mr Kapoor wanted me to ask and to which he wanted to reply: 'No, Mr Kapoor, who built Monte Carlo?'

'I did. I built Monte Carlo!'

'Oh yes, of course.'

'Yes, I built this house, I'm a genius, there's no doubt of it! I have a high opinion of my own opinion, what is yours?'

'Oh, I don't know, but I'm sure you're right.'

'Of course I am. But speak up, don't be afraid to say what you think. Stand up for your rights, even if you're wrong! Throw some more wood on the fire, keep it burning.'

Suddenly Kapoor leapt from my arms and stumbled towards the fire. I shouted out to him, and, catching hold of the end of his green dressing-gown, dragged my host back to safety. Meena Kapoor ran to us and, without so much as a glance at me, took her husband by the arm and propelled him indoors.

I stared after Meena Kapoor, and continued to stare even when she had disappeared. The guests chattered away pleasantly, pretending nothing had happened, keeping the gossip for the next morning, but the children giggled amongst themselves, and the devil Suri shouted:

'Throw some more wood on the fire, keep it burning!'

Somi appeared at my side. 'What did Mr Kapoor have to say?'

'He said he built Monte Carlo.'

Somi slapped his forehead. '*Toba*! Now we'll have to come again tomorrow evening. And then, if he's drunk, we'll have to discuss the matter with his wife, she's the only one with any sense.'

We walked away from the party, out of the circle of fire-light, into the shadows of the banana trees. The voices of the guests became a distant murmur. Suddenly, Suri's high-pitched shout came to us on the clear, still air.

Somi said: 'We must go to the *chaat* shop tomorrow morning, Ranbir is asking for you.'

I had almost forgotten about Ranbir. I felt ashamed for not having asked after him before this. Ranbir was an important person in my life, he had changed the course of my life with nothing but a little colour, red and green, and the touch of his hand.

One day when Ranbir and I were at the *chaat* shop having potato *tikkees* I asked him how Somi and he had become such close friends. They seemed to understand each other so well, trust each other with their lives, and depend on each other in times of need, yet keep a bit of distance between them. I couldn't help but feel envious of such a wonderful friendship, specially since I had no close friends myself.

Ranbir laughingly said, 'Well, you won't believe this, Rusty, but when we first met, Somi and I couldn't stand the sight of each other . . .'

'And then?' I asked.

'Then . . . the pool incident happened.'

I looked at him enquiringly.

'I had been less than a month in Dehra,' said Ranbir, 'when I discovered this pool in the forest. It was the height of summer, and school had not yet opened, and, having made no friends in this place, I wandered about a good deal by myself into the hills and forests. It was hot, very hot, at that time of the year, and as I walked about in my vest and shorts, my brown feet, I remember now, were white with the chalky dust that flew up from the ground. The earth was parched, the grass brown, the trees listless, hardly stirring, waiting for a cool wind or a refreshing shower of rain.

'It was on such a day—a hot, tired day—that I

found the pool in the forest. The water had a gentle translucency, and you could see the smooth round pebbles at the bottom of the pool.

'When I saw the pool, I did not hesitate to get into it. I had often gone swimming, alone or with friends, when I had lived with my parents in a thirsty town in the middle of the Rajputana desert. There, I had known only sticky, muddy pools, where buffaloes wallowed and women washed clothes. I had never seen a pool like this—so clean and cold and inviting . . . I threw off all my clothes, as I had done when I went swimming in the plains, and leapt into the water.

'The next day I went there again to quench my body in the cool waters of the forest pool. I was there for almost an hour, sliding in and out of the limpid green water, or lying stretched out on the smooth yellow rocks in the shade of the broad-leaved sal trees. While I lay like this, naked on a rock, I noticed another boy standing a little distance away, staring at me in a rather hostile manner. A Sikh fellow. I had seen him before in town, but hadn't spoken to him. Not my type, I had thought.

'The boy had only just noticed me, and he stood at the edge of the pool, wearing a pair of bathing shorts, waiting, perhaps, for me to explain myself.

'I did not say anything, and the other called out, "What are you doing here, mister?"

'I had been prepared to be friendly, but was taken aback at the hostility of that fellow's tone.

'"I am swimming," I replied. "Why don't you join me?"

'"I always swim alone," said the other. "This is my pool, I did not invite you here. And why are you not wearing any clothes?"

'"It is not your business if I do not wear clothes. I have nothing to be ashamed of."

'"You fat fellow, put on your clothes."

'"Skinny fool, take yours off."

'I suppose I had provoked him too much. He strode up to me—I was still sitting on the rock—and, planting his broad feet firmly on the sand, said (as though this would settle the matter once and for all), "Don't you know I am a Punjabi? I do not take replies from loafers like you!"

'"So you like to fight with loafers?" I asked. "Well, I am not a loafer. I am a Rajput!"

'"I am a Punjabi!"

'"I am a Rajput!"

'We had reached an impasse. There was little else that could be said.

'"You understand that I am a Punjabi?" said the stranger, feeling that perhaps this information had not penetrated my head, for I was still sitting there coolly.

'"I have heard you say it three times," I replied.

'"Then why are you not running away?"

'"I am waiting for *you* to run away!"

'"I will have to beat you," said the stranger, assuming a violent attitude, showing me the palm of his hand.

'"I am waiting to see you do it," I said.

'"You will see me do it," said the other boy.

'Well, I waited,' said Ranbir. 'The other boy made a strange, hissing sound. We stared each other in the eye for almost a minute. Then the Punjabi boy slapped me across the face with all the force he could muster. I staggered, feeling quite dizzy. I saw later that there were thick red finger marks on my cheek.

'"There you are!" exclaimed my assailant. "Will you be off now?"

'I was so furious at that skinny fellow's gall to slap me that I swung my arm up and pushed a hard, bony fist into the other's face.'

'Then what happened, Ranbir?' I asked. My last potato *tikkee* was getting cold on the banana leaf. I was so mesmerized by Ranbir's storytelling that I had stopped eating.

'Then the obvious happened, Rusty. We were at each other's throats, swaying on the rock, tumbling on to the sand, rolling over and over, our legs and arms locked in a desperate, violent struggle. Gasping and cursing, clawing and slapping, we rolled right into the shallows of the pool.

'Even in the water the fight continued as, spluttering and covered with mud, we groped for each other's head and throat. But after five minutes of frenzied, unscientific struggle, neither of us had emerged victorious. Our bodies heaving with exhaustion, we stood back from each other, making tremendous efforts to speak.

'"Now—now do you realize—I am a Punjabi?" gasped the stranger.

'"Do you know I am a Rajput?"

'We gave a moment's consideration to each other's answers and, in that moment of silence, there was only our heavy breathing to be heard.

'"Then you will not leave the pool?" said the Punjabi boy.

'"I will not leave it," I said stoutly.

'"Then we shall have to continue the fight," said the other.

'"All right," I said—I wasn't going to give in so easily.

'But neither of us moved, neither took the initiative. The Punjabi boy had an inspiration.

'"We will continue the fight tomorrow," he said. "If you dare to come here again tomorrow, we will continue this fight, and I will not show you mercy as I have done today."

183

'"I will come tomorrow," I said. "I will be ready for you."

'We turned from each other then and, going to our respective rocks, put on our clothes, and left the forest by different routes.'

I was surprised at two things—the antagonism between Somi and Ranbir when they first met, and Ranbir's capability to narrate the encounter so well.

So eloquent and articulate was he that I could picturize in my mind every little detail in that scene. It was like watching a movie being played just for me. 'So did you both meet the next day as well, Ranbir? Don't stop, just continue with what happened next!'

By now Ranbir was also hugely enjoying himself. He was itching to tell me the rest. 'Well, when I got home, I found it difficult to explain the cuts and bruises that showed on my face, legs and arms. It was difficult to conceal the fact that I had been in an unusually violent fight, and my mother insisted on my staying at home for the rest of the day. That evening, though, I slipped out of the house and went to the bazaar, where I found comfort and solace in a bottle of vividly-coloured lemonade and a banana-leaf full of hot, sweet *jalebi*s. I had just finished the lemonade when I saw my adversary coming down the road. My first impulse was to turn away and look elsewhere, my second to throw the lemonade bottle at my enemy. But I did neither of these things. Instead, I stood my ground and scowled at the fellow. He said nothing either, but scowled back with equal ferocity.

'The next day was as hot as the previous one. I felt weak and lazy, Rusty, and not at all eager for a fight. My body was stiff and sore after the previous day's encounter. But I could not refuse the challenge. Not to turn up at the pool would be an acknowledgement of defeat. Frankly speaking, from the way I felt just then, I knew I would be beaten in another fight. But I could not acquiesce in my own defeat. I had to defy my enemy to the last, or outwit him, for only then could I gain his respect. If I surrendered at that point, I would be beaten for all time, but to fight and be beaten today left me free to fight and be beaten again. As long as I fought, I had a right to the pool in the forest.

'I was half hoping that the Punjabi boy would have forgotten the challenge, but these hopes were dashed when I saw my opponent sitting, stripped to the waist, on a rock on the other side of the pool. He was rubbing oil on his body, massaging it into his thighs. He saw me beneath the sal trees, and called a challenge across the waters of the pool.

'"Come over to this side and fight!" he shouted.

'But I was not going to submit to any conditions laid down by my opponent.

'"Come *this* side and fight!" I shouted back with equal vigour.

'"Swim across and fight me here!" called the other. "Or perhaps you cannot swim the length of this pool?"

'He didn't know then that I am a wrestler, and that at any given time I can swim the length of that pool a dozen times without tiring. I felt that this was a good opportunity to show the Punjabi boy my superiority. So, slipping out of my vest and shorts, I dived straight into the water, cutting through it like a knife, and surfaced with hardly a splash. My adversary's mouth hung open in amazement. Obviously, I had scored a point.

'"You can dive!" he exclaimed.

'"It is easy," I said casually, treading water, waiting for a further challenge. "Can't you dive?"

'"No," said the other. "I jump straight in. But if you will tell me how, I will make a dive."

'"It is easy," I said. "Stand on the rock, stretch your arms out and allow your head to displace your feet."

'The Punjabi boy stood up, stiff and straight, stretched out his arms, and threw himself into the water. He landed flat on his belly, with a crash that sent the birds screaming out of the trees.

'I just dissolved into laughter.

"'Are you trying to empty the pool?" I asked him as he came to the surface, spouting water like a small whale.

"'Wasn't it good?" he asked me, evidently proud of his feat.

"'Not very good. You should have more practice. See, I will do it again." And I executed another perfect dive. He waited for me to come up, but, swimming underwater, I circled him and came upon him from behind.

"'How did you do that?" he asked, astonished.

"'Can't you swim underwater?" I asked.

"'No, but I will try it. Will you teach me?"

"'If you like, I will teach you."

"'You must teach me. If you do not teach me, I will beat you. Will you come here every day and teach me?"

"'If you like," I replied. We pulled ourselves out of the water, and sat side by side on a smooth grey rock.

"'My name is Somi," said the Punjabi boy. "What is yours?"

"'It is Ranbir."

"'You are strong," said Somi. "You are a real *pahelwan*."

"'Yes, I wrestle quite a bit," I said. "One day I will be the world's champion wrestler. You are quite strong yourself, Somi," I conceded. "But you are too bony. I know, you people do not eat enough. You must come and have your food with me. I drink one seer of milk every day. We have got our own cow! Be my friend, and I will make you a *pahelwan* like me!"

'Somi put his arm around my shoulders and said, "We are friends now, yes?" And in that moment love and understanding were born between us. "We are friends," I agreed.

'"Now this is our pool," said Somi. "Nobody else can come here without our permission. Who would dare?"

'Who would indeed, Rusty? We make a super team—Somi and I. Today everyone is envious of our friendship, but very few know that it is that beautiful, cool green pool in the forest which brought us together.'

I felt curiously content after hearing this long story from Ranbir. In the company of such true and good friends, life seemed to be beautiful and the world a happier place to live in. 'Let's celebrate!' I said, and ordered another round of tikkees.

A couple of days later, Ranbir, Somi and I were seated in the *chaat* shop, discussing my situation. Ranbir looked miserable; his hair fell sadly over his forehead, and he shied away from looking me straight in the eye.

'I have got you into trouble,' he apologized gruffly, 'I am too ashamed.'

I laughed. After licking the sauce off my fingers and crumpling up my empty leaf bowl, I admonished him, 'Silly fellow, for what are you sorry? For making me happy? For taking me away from my guardian? Well, I am not sorry, you can be sure of that'

'You are not angry?' asked Ranbir in wonder.

'No, but you will make me angry if you go on moping this way.' Ranbir's face lit up, and he slapped my back with a sudden enthusiasm and said, 'Come on, misters, I am going to make you sick with *gol-guppas* so that you won't be able to eat any more until I return from Mussoorie!'

'Mussoorie?' Somi looked puzzled. 'You are going to Mussoorie?'

'To school!'

'That's right,' said a voice from the door, a voice hidden in smoke. 'Now we've had it . . .'

Somi whispered, 'It's that monkey-millionaire Kishen! He's come to make a nuisance of himself.' Then, louder: 'Come over here, Kishen, come and join us in *gol-guppas*!'

Kishen appeared from the mist of vapour, walking with an affected swagger, his hands in his pockets; he was the only one present wearing pants instead of pyjamas.

'Hey!' exclaimed Somi, 'who has given you a black eye?'

Kishen did not answer immediately, but sat down opposite me. His shirt hung over his pants, and his pants hung over his knees. He had bushy eyebrows and hair, and a drooping, disagreeable mouth; the sulky expression on his face had become a permanent one, not a mood of the moment. Kishen's swagger, money, unattractive face and qualities made him curiously attractive, at least, that's what I thought . . . Anyway, it didn't matter to me whether Kishen swaggered consciously, whether he had money or possessed an unattractive face. As far as I was concerned, he was the boy who I was to tutor, and with whose father's money I was to survive.

He prodded his nose with his forefinger, as he always did when a trifle excited. 'Those damn wrestlers, they piled on to me.'

'Why?' said Ranbir, sitting up instantly.

'I was making a badminton court on the *maidan*, and these fellows came along and said they had reserved the place for a wrestling ground.'

'So then?'

Kishen's affected American twang—I don't know how he even came to have such an accent—became more pronounced. 'I told them to go to hell!'

Ranbir laughed. 'So they all started wrestling you?'

'Yeah, but I didn't know they would hit me too. I

bet if you fellows were there, they wouldn't have tried anything. Isn't that so, Ranbir?'

Ranbir smiled; he knew it was so, but did not care to speak of his physical prowess. Kishen took notice of me suddenly.

'Are you Mister Rusty?' he asked.

'Yes, I am,' I replied and for the lack of anything else to say, asked, 'are you Mister Kishen?'

'I am Mister Kishen. You know how to box, Rusty?'

'Well,' I said, unwilling to become involved in a local feud, 'I've never boxed wrestlers.'

Somi changed the subject. 'Rusty's coming to see your father this evening. You must try and persuade your pop to give him the job of teaching you English.'

Kishen prodded his nose, and gave me a sly wink. 'Yes, Daddy told me about you, he says you are a professor. You can be my teacher on the condition that we don't work too hard, and that you support me when I tell them lies, and that you tell them I am working hard. Sure, you can be my teacher, sure . . . better you than a real one.'

'I'll try to please everyone,' I said.

'You're a clever person if you can. But I think you *are* clever.'

'Yes,' I agreed, and was inwardly amazed at the way I spoke.

Somi then suggested that the two of us—Kishen and I—should go to Kishen's house together. So that evening, I met Kishen in the bazaar and walked home with him.

There was a crowd in front of the bazaar's only cinema, and it was getting restive and demonstrative.

One had to fight to get into this particular cinema, as there was no organized queuing or booking.

'Is anything wrong?' I asked.

'Oh, no,' said Kishen, 'it is just Laurel and Hardy today, they are very popular. Whenever a popular film is shown, there is usually a riot. But I know of a way in through the roof, I'll show you some time.'

'Sounds crazy.'

'Yeah, the roof leaks, so people usually bring their umbrellas. Also their food, because when the projector breaks down or the electricity fails, we have to wait a long time. Sometimes, when it is a long wait, the *chaat-wallah* comes in and does some business.'

'Sounds crazy,' I repeated.

'You'll get used to it. Have a chewing gum.' Kishen's jaws had been working incessantly on a lump of gum that had been increasing in size over the last three days; he started on a fresh stick every hour or so, without throwing away the old ones. I was used to seeing Indians chew *paan,* the betel-leaf preparation which stained the mouth with red juices, but Kishen wasn't like any of the Indians I had met so far. I accepted a stick of gum, and we walked home in silent concentration, our jaws moving rhythmically, and Kishen's tongue making sudden sucking sounds.

As we entered the front room, Meena Kapoor pounced on Kishen.

'Ah! So you have decided to come home at last! And what do you mean by asking Daddy for money without letting me know? What have you done with it, Kishen? Where is it?'

Kishen sauntered across the room and deposited himself on the couch. 'I've spent it.'

Mrs Kapoor's hands went to her hips. 'What do you mean, you've spent it!'

'I mean I've eaten it.'

He got two resounding slaps across his face, and his flesh went white where his mother's fingers left their mark. I backed towards the door hurriedly; it was embarrassing to be present at this intimate family scene.

'Don't go, Rusty,' shouted Kishen, 'or she won't stop slapping me!'

Kapoor, still wearing his green dressing-gown and beard, came in from the adjoining room, and his wife turned on him.

'Why do you give the child so much money?' she

demanded. 'You know he spends it on nothing but bazaar food and makes himself sick.'

I seized at the opportunity of pleasing the whole family—of saving Mr Kapoor's skin, pacifying his wife, and gaining the affection and regard of Kishen.

'It is all my fault,' I said, 'I took Kishen to the *chaat* shop. I'm very sorry.'

Meena Kapoor became quiet and her eyes softened; but I resented her kindly expression because I knew it was prompted by pity—pity for me—and a satisfied pride. Mrs Kapoor was proud because she thought her son had shared his money with one who apparently hadn't any.

'I did not see you come in,' she said.

'I only wanted to explain about the money.'

'Come in, don't be shy.'

Her smile was full of kindness, but I was not looking for kindness. For no apparent reason, I felt lonely; I missed Somi, felt lost without him, helpless and clumsy.

'There is another thing,' I said, remembering the post of professor in English.

'But come in, Mister Rusty . . .'

It was the first time she had used my name, and the gesture immediately placed us on equal terms. She was a graceful woman, much younger than Kapoor; her features had a clear classic beauty, and her voice was gentle but firm. Her hair was tied in a neat bun and laced with a string of jasmine flowers.

'Come in . . .'

'About teaching Kishen . . .' I mumbled, not knowing what else to say.

'Come and play carom,' said Kishen from the couch. 'We are none of us any good. Come and sit down, pardner.'

'He fancies himself as an American,' said Mrs Kapoor. 'If ever you see him in the cinema, drag him out.'

The carom board was brought in from the next room, and it was arranged that Mr Kapoor and I would be partners. We began to play, but the game didn't progress very fast because Kapoor kept leaving the table in order to disappear behind a screen, from the direction of which came a tinkle of bottles and glasses. I started getting apprehensive about Kapoor getting drunk before he could be approached about the job of teaching Kishen.

'My wife,' said Kapoor in a loud whisper to me, 'does not let me drink in public any more, so I have to do it in a cupboard.'

He looked sad. There were tear stains on his cheeks; the tears were caused not by his wife's scolding, which he ignored, but by his own self-pity. Somi had told me that Mr Kapoor often cried for himself, usually in his sleep.

Whenever I pocketed one of the carom men, Kapoor exclaimed: 'Ah, nice shot, nice shot!' as though it were a cricket match we were playing. 'But hit it slowly, slowly . . .' And when it was his turn, he gave the striker a feeble push, moving it a bare inch from his finger.

'Play properly,' murmured Mrs Kapoor, who was intent on winning the game, but Kapoor would be up from his seat again, and the company would sit back and wait for the tune of clinking glass.

It was a very irritating game. Kapoor insisted on showing me how to strike the men, and whenever I made a mistake, Mrs Kapoor said 'thank you' in an amused and conceited manner that angered me. When she and Kishen had cleared the board of whites, Kapoor and I were left with eight blacks.

'Thank you,' said Mrs Kapoor sweetly.

'We are too good for you,' scoffed Kishen, busily arranging the board for another game.

Kapoor took sudden interest in the proceedings: 'Who won, I say, who won?'

Much to my disgust, another game was started, and with the same partners, but we had just started to play when Kapoor flopped forward and knocked the carom board off the table. He had fallen asleep. I took him by the shoulders and eased him back into the chair. Kapoor's breathing was heavy; saliva had collected at the sides of his mouth, and he snorted a little.

I thought it was time I left. Rising from the table, I said, 'I will have to ask another time about the job . . .'

'Hasn't he told you as yet?' said Kishen's mother.

'What?'

'That you can have the job.'

'Can I!'

She gave a little laugh. 'But of course! Certainly there is no one else who would take it on, Kishen is not easy to teach. There is no fixed pay, but we will give you anything you need. You are not our servant. You will be doing us a favour by giving Kishen some of your knowledge and conversation and company, and in return we will be giving you our hospitality. You will have a room of your own, and your food you will have with us. What do you think?'

'Oh, it is wonderful!' I said.

And it was wonderful, and I felt gay and light-headed, and it looked like all the troubles in the world had scurried away: I even felt successful—I had a profession.

And Meena Kapoor was smiling at me, and looking more beautiful than she really was, and Kishen was saying:

'Tomorrow you must stay till twelve o'clock, all right, even if Daddy goes to sleep. Promise me?'

'Promise.'

I saw an unaffected enthusiasm bubbling up in Kishen. It was quite different to the sulkiness of his usual manner. I had liked him in spite of his unattractive qualities, and now liked him more, for Kishen had taken me into his home and confidence without knowing me very well and without asking any questions. Kishen was a scoundrel, a monkey—crude and well-spoilt—but, for him to have taken a liking to me (and I held myself in high esteem), he must have some virtues . . . or so I reasoned.

While I walked back to Somi's house, I dwelt on my relationship with Kishen, but my tongue, when I loosened it in Somi's presence, dwelt on Meena Kapoor. And when I lay down to sleep, I saw her in my mind's eye, and for the first time took conscious note of her beauty, of her warmth and softness, and made up my mind that I would fall in love with her.